'I'm a docto
known someth

Her mouth trembled as she spoke, pressed her lips together to stop it from happening.

'It isn't your fault,' Jordan said firmly.

'Even so, I can't help feeling that I'm to blame.' Her eyes flooded with tears again, and he reached up and gently brushed them away with his thumb. Then, out of the blue, he tilted her chin with his cupped hand and dropped a tender kiss on her parted lips.

She stared at him in startled wonder. He had kissed her. Jordan had kissed her and it seemed as though the world had suddenly stopped its spinning and she was floating in suspended animation.

A&E DRAMA

Blood pressure is high and pulses are racing in these fast-paced, dramatic stories from Mills & Boon® Medical Romance™. They'll move a mountain to save a life in an emergency, be they the crash team, ER doctors, fire, air or land rescue paramedics. There are lots of critical engagements amongst the high tensions and emotional passions in these exciting stories of lives and loves at risk!

A&E DRAMA

Hearts are racing!

A CONSULTANT'S SPECIAL CARE

BY
JOANNA NEIL

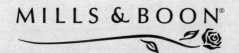

MILLS & BOON®

*All the characters in this book have no existence outside the imagination
of the author, and have no relation whatsoever to anyone bearing the
same name or names. They are not even distantly inspired by any
individual known or unknown to the author, and all the incidents are
pure invention.*

*First published in Great Britain 2003
Harlequin Mills & Boon Limited,
Eton House, 18-24 Paradise Road, Richmond, Surrey TW9 1SR*

© Joanna Neil 2003

ISBN 0 263 83476 X

*Set in Times Roman 10½ on 12 pt.
03-1003-51402*

*Printed and bound in Spain
by Litografía Rosés, S.A., Barcelona*

CHAPTER ONE

'HELP... Oh, please, help me, someone. I think he's hurt badly...he can't breathe...'

Abby heard the distressed cry from where she was sitting, on a sun-warmed golden stretch of sand in the lee of an outcrop of rocks. She had been watching the holidaymakers swimming in the sea, enjoying the rare peace of a summer's afternoon while she listened to the snatches of laughter and sounds of children playing nearby.

Now, though, the tranquillity of the day was abruptly shattered. Abby lifted a hand to shield her eyes from the sun and looked over to where the appeal had come from, further along the cove, where a craggy promontory jutted out into the sea, its rock-strewn base dashed by increasingly powerful waves. A fair-haired young woman was kneeling on the beach, and she appeared to be cradling a man in her arms.

Instinct took over, and Abby scrambled to her feet as quickly as she could, snatching up her sandals and canvas bag. The skirt of her cotton dress flapped against her bare legs as she went, creating a faint breeze that cooled her hot skin as she hurried along the shoreline towards the couple.

Reaching them, she saw that the man wasn't moving, but was simply lying there as though he had collapsed. He was in his early twenties, she guessed, on the thin side, his body still damp from swimming in the sea, and there were fresh grazes on his chest. Looking at them, Abby frowned.

'I heard you call. What happened? What's wrong?' she asked, sinking down on to the sand beside the pair. The mass of her honey gold curls fell across her cheek with the movement, clouding her vision, and she swept them away with the palm of her hand, tucking the silky strands behind her ear.

'He was swimming, and I think he was beginning to get tired,' the girl said shakily. 'He's been ill recently—a kind of flu virus, I think… I knew he was overdoing it and I told him he should stop, but he wouldn't listen…I don't know what he was trying to prove. The waves were getting fiercer and I said we should be going.' Her mouth was trembling, her voice breaking in panic.

'Then all of a sudden a huge wave came and took him by surprise and toppled him over and he was too close to the rocks. I knew he was too close. I think he stumbled and he must have fallen onto them. He was winded—I could see that. It was all he could do to get back to me, and then he collapsed…' She looked up at Abby, her blue eyes troubled, on the verge of tears. 'I don't know what to do. I need to get help, but I can't leave him like this.'

'I'm a doctor,' Abby said, her gaze busily moving over the ashen-faced man. 'I'll have a look at him, shall I?'

She said it confidently enough, but if the truth were known, she had not long ago finished a stint as a house officer, and she was still feeling a little unsure of herself. Her next post as senior house officer wasn't due to start until tomorrow and even that threatened to be a nerve-racking experience.

She hadn't met her new boss yet, but Mr Blakesley's reputation had gone before him. He was known to be sometimes curt, blunt and demanding, and as the consultant in charge of Accident and Emergency at the Roseland Hospital, he was the one who would be supervising her experience of emergency medicine for the next six months.

Pushing those awkward thoughts aside, she concentrated her attention on the injured man. He was still conscious, but he appeared to be in pain and wasn't paying either of them very much attention just then. 'What's his name?'

'Kieran. I'm Vicky. We just came down here for the weekend. We thought Cornwall would be so romantic…' Her voice trailed off in despair.

Abby tried to reassure her patient. 'Kieran,' she murmured gently, 'I'm Dr Curtis—Abby. I'm going to take care of you, but I just need to examine you for a moment. Is that all right with you?'

Kieran nodded, almost imperceptibly, as though the effort was too great, and Abby quickly checked his pulse. His breathing was laboured, and she looked carefully down at the grazed area of his chest. She watched as he tried to breathe and discovered that there was a part of his rib cage that wasn't rising and falling as it should. Instead of expanding as he breathed in, that section moved inwards, and when he tried to expel the air from his chest, it shifted outwards.

'I think you have what we call a flail chest,' Abby explained to him quietly. 'It means that you've probably broken several of your ribs in a couple of places, so that part of the rib cage is moving independently and interfering with your breathing. I'll do what I can to make you feel more comfortable, and then we'll get you moved to hospital for a proper check-up.'

She lifted her gaze to Vicky. 'I'll need to go and get my medical bag from my car,' she said softly. 'I'll be just a couple of minutes…it isn't too far away. Will you watch him carefully while I'm gone? Don't move him at all, just make sure that he's comfortable and try to keep him warm. If he should stop breathing, tilt his head back slightly and blow into his mouth. Do you think you can do that?'

Vicky looked at her with frightened eyes, but she nodded all the same.

'OK, then.' Abby looked around and saw that there was a beach towel spread out on the sand nearby. 'We'll cover him with this, shall we?'

She carefully tucked the towel around Kieran, and then got to her feet, reaching into her bag for her phone to call for an ambulance as she headed towards the cliff. Her car was parked on a standing space on the clifftop, and she was thankful that she was strong and healthy and could manage the climb at a reasonable pace. She wasn't so sure that the ambulance crew would cope as well in this terrain with a patient on a stretcher, though, and when the operator suggested sending the rescue helicopter, Abby agreed readily enough.

Going back down to the beach was more difficult when she was carrying her medical kit, but she made as much haste as was possible, knowing that Kieran's condition could deteriorate at any moment. He was already having problems with his breathing, and if he had punctured a lung or a blood vessel, he could be in deep trouble.

'He's getting worse.' Vicky's agitated words greeted

Abby as she came to kneel down beside her patient once more. 'What's the matter with him? Can you help him?'

By now Kieran was showing clear signs that something was very wrong with him. His breathing was rapid and his lips were beginning to show a bluish tinge. 'He needs oxygen,' Abby murmured.

Quickly, she slid a Guedel airway into place, and then covered his mouth and nose with a face mask and began to squeeze the attached ventilation bag. 'Do you think you could manage to do this?' she asked Vicky. 'I need to examine him again.' As she spoke, she heard the gratifying drone of the rescue helicopter in the distance. At least help wasn't far away.

'Yes, I can do that.'

'Good.' Abby ran her stethoscope over Kieran's chest. There were no breath sounds on his injured side and he was becoming increasingly distressed. His pulse was rapid, and the veins in his neck were becoming distended, and all that was very bad news. It meant that pressure was building up dangerously, and if she didn't act soon, he could go into cardiac arrest.

'Kieran,' she said gently, 'the injury has caused a tear in the pleural cavity around your lungs, and air is building up in there because it can't escape. That's why you're having difficulty breathing. It's caused your lung to collapse, and I need to relieve the pressure by putting in a tube. I'm going to give you an anaesthetic so that it won't hurt as I do that.'

His situation was desperate, and she worked as fast as she could, sliding a cannula between his ribs and withdrawing the needle. There was a reassuring hiss of air as the gas escaped, and she taped the cannula in place and inserted a chest drain. In the background, she could hear the whir of the helicopter blades as it approached.

A paramedic came to stand beside her a few minutes later. 'What's the situation here?'

She looked up and greeted him with a feeling of relief. Briefly, Abby outlined the patient's condition.

'OK,' he said when she had finished. 'My partner and I will get him aboard the helicopter and then I'll let the hospital know that we're coming in.'

His partner was already preparing the stretcher. 'I'd like to go with him,' Abby said quickly. 'His condition could worsen, and I want to do what I can for him. I feel responsible for monitoring him, since I've already been giving him treatment.'

'That's all right.' The paramedic smiled and glanced at Vicky, waiting anxiously by Kieran's side. 'We've room enough for two more.' He helped secure their patient on the stretcher. 'It'll take us about ten minutes to get there, but Dr Blakesley and his team will be ready for us.'

Abby felt a quiver of alarm run through her. It was beginning to look as though she was going to meet her new boss sooner than she had expected. She could only hope that the meeting would go well.

She looked on while the paramedics transferred Kieran by stretcher to the helicopter, which was waiting some distance away. When he was safely installed, the paramedic in charge helped Vicky climb in alongside Kieran, and Abby followed.

She wasn't at all happy with her patient's pallor, and as the helicopter took off and the journey progressed, she realised that he was showing increasing signs of distress. That was very worrying.

Vicky held his hand and murmured soothing words, while Abby inwardly fretted. If anything, he should be showing signs of his condition improving, but instead he was experiencing increased breathlessness and his pulse rate was rising. She glanced at the chest drain, and doubts crept into her mind.

If only she knew more about emergency medicine. Although she had followed what she believed was correct procedure, it wasn't beyond the realms of possibility that she had made a mistake somewhere along the way.

'He's still breathless,' the paramedic observed, and Abby nodded. Could she have pushed the tube in too far?

The paramedic quietly relayed the developments back to the hospital via his radio and listened to the response. 'Dr Blakesley is going to meet us as soon as we land,' he told Abby. 'His team will be standing by.'

His words were meant to be reassuring, but Abby had mixed feelings about that. What would Mr Blakesley think of her if she had messed things up? With her patient in poor condition there was the distinct possibility that she could find herself starting off on the wrong foot with her new boss.

She glanced back at her patient. If blood was building up in his pleural cavity, he was in imminent danger... She found herself praying that they would get to the hospital very soon. It was more than likely that Kieran would need surgery to repair the wound in his chest.

'We'll need to send blood for cross-matching,' she said. 'I'll organise that now...and we'll start intravenous fluids.' That should compensate in part for what Kieran was losing.

They landed a few minutes later, and Mr Blakesley was taking charge even before Abby had stepped down from the helicopter. While the paramedics were giving their report, Abby stood back and had time to observe the consultant momentarily.

Somehow, he wasn't at all what she had expected. He was relatively young, for a start, in his mid-thirties, she guessed, long-limbed, and full of vital energy, his jet-black hair tousled by the wind from the whirling rotor blades of the helicopter. He was wearing an expensively tailored grey suit, the jacket open to reveal a dark blue shirt.

Within seconds Kieran had been transferred to a trolley and then he was being whisked off through the wide doors of the hospital and along a corridor to-wards A and E.

Abby hurried to keep up. 'He's losing too much blood,' she said worriedly, coming alongside Mr Blakesley. 'He must have lost two litres already.'

The consultant was giving instructions to his team as they went, ordering X-rays and tests and calling for a cardiothoracic surgeon, but he paused long enough to throw her a quick glance.

Close up, his features were even more impressive than she had at first noticed, and she was thrown com-pletely off guard for a moment or two. He was in-credibly good-looking, his face angular, strong-jawed, his compelling eyes a satisfying mixture of blue and grey. His mouth was firmly moulded...attractively masculine, she thought distractedly, and immediately berated herself. How could she allow such an irrelevant observation to creep into her thoughts at a time like this?

'I know you must be concerned,' he said briefly, 'but I can assure you that we'll take very good care of him.' His voice was deep and resonant, his tone reassuring. His gaze shifted to take in Vicky, who had paused uncertainly alongside Abby and was looking anxious and tearful. 'For the moment,' he added, 'it would probably be for the best if you let the nurse show you both to a waiting room while we look after him. We'll let you know how he is as soon as we can.'

Unsure of herself and bewildered by events, Vicky allowed the nurse to gently lead her away, and Abby heard her asking what was happening to Kieran, and what his chances of recovery were. Abby stayed where she was, following Mr Blakesley into the emergency room. 'You don't understand,' she began, and he lifted a querying brow.

'Are you a relative?' he asked, and she realised with a small frown of dismay that he must believe that the doctor who had treated Kieran had stayed behind at the beach. He went on, 'I know that Miss Baxter is his girlfriend, but perhaps you would like to tell me who you are?'

He looked her over fleetingly, and she was suddenly conscious of the flimsy summer dress she was wearing, a sunny yellow cotton creation, splashed here and there with a pattern of tiny pale flowers. The bodice clung to her curves and emphasised her slender waist, leaving her shoulders bare except for two narrow straps, and the skirt draped itself around her legs, falling in gentle folds to her knees.

His glance flicked to the shimmering cloud of wayward curls that tumbled around her face and lightly brushed her shoulders. Abby's cheeks flushed with hot colour. She must look like a dishevelled tourist when, more than anything else, she needed to appear calm and professional.

'I…I'm Abby Curtis,' she explained awkwardly. 'Dr Curtis. I'm the one who treated him at the beach.' Hesitantly, she added, 'He was suffering from a tension pneumothorax and I had to act quickly. I'm… I'm just afraid I may have pushed the drain in a little too far.'

His blue-grey eyes widened a fraction and held her gaze for a second or two. 'Abby Curtis,' he echoed thoughtfully, adding in an enquiring undertone, 'So…are you the one who's about to become a new member of my team?'

Abby nodded in response. 'That's right. I am.'

His mouth made a faint, ironic twist. 'And you think you could be responsible for the fact that our patient is bleeding to death? That's quite an afternoon's work, Dr Curtis.'

He paused momentarily, then flicked a glance at Kieran, adding, 'I believe my patient needs me right now. As I said, perhaps you had better take some time out while we take a look at him and see what needs to be done. You've done your bit, and from the looks of him it will take some time to put right whatever has gone wrong. I need to find out what exactly is causing the bleeding, and I suggest that you leave me to get on with it.'

Abby felt the colour drain from her face. She was sure her mouth must have dropped open at his words, and her only consolation was that at least he was no longer there to witness her humiliation. He was striding purposefully across the room towards a treatment bay and she was left standing there, suffering from an acute attack of dismay.

One of the male doctors on his team threw her a quick glance and winced in sympathy, before turning to the patient.

Slowly, Abby pulled herself together. What was it that she had expected from the consultant—a few words of comfort, perhaps, for him to say that Kieran was safe now that they had him in hospital? And maybe an explanation of how these things came about and what could be done to avoid them happening again? A teaching insight, maybe…was that what she had been hoping for, among other things? After all, she was due to start her posting at this hospital to-morrow, under Mr Blakesley's guidance, and surely, at the least, she could have looked forward to some measure of support from him.

It didn't seem as though she was going to get any of that, though, did it? Unhappily, she absorbed that fact, and then slowly stiffened her back, cementing her resolve. She had acted in good faith when she had gone to help Kieran, had done everything she could to keep him alive. No one, not even the all-powerful consultant, Mr Blakesley, was going to put her down for long. She was here to learn, and she would do everything in her power to become a good doctor, in spite of his abrupt dismissal of her.

For the time being, she went to find Vicky in the waiting room.

'Is there any news?' Vicky asked, but Abby shook her head.

'Not yet, I'm afraid. It will take a while. They'll do scans to find out the extent of his injuries, and then the surgeon will most likely take over. I'm sure Mr Blakesley will do everything for him that can be done—he's a very-well respected consultant.'

No matter what her immediate opinion of him was, she had to give him that. Abby had heard about Jordan Blakesley from a number of different sources, and though his manner might leave something to be desired, they had all spoken well of his medical expertise. That was why she had applied for this new posting.

In truth, she had ignored the fact that some people commented that he sometimes had an abrasive manner and that he could be difficult at times, because she had imagined that was just hearsay. She wanted to learn alongside the very best, and she was prepared to accept a few foibles.

She had interpreted their comments to mean that he probably didn't suffer fools gladly, but she certainly hadn't imagined that she might find herself in that awkward position from the outset. It was only now that she was beginning to have doubts about the wisdom of her choice.

Eventually a nurse came to tell them about Kieran's condition. She spoke gently to Vicky, telling her that she could go and see him in the intensive care unit.

Abby didn't want to intrude on their privacy. Instead, she decided to go and get herself a cup of coffee from the machine in the corridor. Perhaps she would get to hear what had happened to him if she hung around for a bit longer.

What she wasn't expecting was that Jordan Blakesley would come along and find her burning her fingers on the hot coffee that spilled as she lifted the plastic cup. She licked her fingers to help ease the sting and immediately felt embarrassed to be caught that way.

'So you're still here, Dr Curtis,' he murmured. 'Worried about what you might have done to that young man, are you?'

Her green eyes sparked fitfully and then narrowed on him. 'Of course I'm concerned about how he is. Isn't that only natural?' There was a hint of tension in her voice as she went on, 'I did what I could for him. I did my best, but if I made a mistake, I feel really badly about that.'

'Do you? And have you been waiting here, all this time, going over everything that might have gone wrong?'

Abby bit her lip and put her coffee cup down. 'I don't know why you're giving me such a hard time over this,' she said, her chin lifting. 'I was looking for support from you, since you're about to become my mentor. I hadn't bargained for outright condemnation.'

He lifted a dark brow. 'You think I was harsh in my judgement of you?'

She had probably already burned her boats, so she went for the truth. 'I do.'

His mouth quirked momentarily, and she thought she saw a glint of humour in his eyes, but it passed so suddenly that she decided she must have imagined it. 'Well, at least you speak your mind,' he said abruptly, frowning at her. 'That's something, I suppose.'

Had she gone too far? Doubts suddenly crowded in on her. 'I've not had a lot of experience in emergency medicine,' she said, backing down a little. 'And some of what I did was what I had only learned in theory. I didn't know that I would be thrown into things at the deep end, so to speak. I was rather hoping that my next few months as a senior house officer would help me to improve my skills. '

'Being thrown in at the deep end is what happens in A and E,' he remarked brusquely. 'None of us can know every type of incident that will come our way, but we have to learn how to deal with it.' He sent her a hard blue stare. 'If you're going to be part of my team, you're going to have to learn to be a lot more confident about the decisions you make, and not be forever looking back on yourself to see where you went wrong.'

'I realise that... I thought—I hoped that would come with time.'

'I hope so, too, Dr Curtis. For all our sakes.' His glance seared her. 'In fact, you should know that you saved the man's life. His injuries caused a haemothorax, which led to him losing a lot of blood, and you did what you could to compensate for that. The surgeon has dealt with the tear and managed to stem the bleeding. He'll be all right.'

A surge of relief flooded through her. 'Oh, I'm so glad about that.'

'Of course. We all are.' His glance ran fleetingly over her, making her conscious all over again of her beach clothes. 'Are you expected somewhere, or do you have time to take a look at him?'

'I don't have to rush back just yet. I've a few things that I must see to at home, and I'll need to go and pick up my car fairly soon—I left it on the clifftop— but, yes, I'd like to go and see him, if that's all right.'

He nodded. 'You had better come with me, then,

and take a look at the results of your handiwork.'
Without any more preamble, he moved briskly away.

Abby blinked, feeling somehow as though she had
just been in collision with a juggernaut. Then, seeing
his tall figure rapidly disappearing along the corridor,
she got a grip on herself and hurried after him.

She had never before come across anyone who was
such a peculiar mixture of abrasiveness and compelling vigour...except perhaps for her ex-boyfriend,
Richard. He had certainly been one to make decisions
and sweep her along with him, hadn't he?

He hadn't started out that way, though. To begin
with, he had simply been kind and considerate, wanting only to please her. It had only been later that his
strength of will had emerged and eventually turned to
something infinitely more disquieting.

Catching up with the consultant, Abby went with
him into the intensive-care unit. Kieran was asleep,
his body needing rest after the trauma he had gone
through. His vital signs were being monitored, and
there were tubes and drips of various sorts attached
to him to support his recovery. Vicky sat beside his
bed, and she looked up and smiled as the two of them
came into the room.

'The nurses said they think he's going to be all
right.'

'I know,' Abby said softly. 'I'm glad.'

'He's still drowsy from the anaesthetic,' Jordan put
in, 'but his vital signs have improved, and he seems
to be doing well enough. The tubes can probably
come out in a day or so.'

They stayed by his bedside for a moment or two,
while Jordan explained to Vicky about Kieran's condition and told her what was likely to happen next.

Then he signalled to Abby that it was time to leave, and they said goodbye and quietly left the room.

Out in the corridor, Jordan looked down at the gold watch on his wrist. 'I have to go. That's my stint finished for the day, and I'm due at a charity function within the hour.' He threw her a quick look. 'You said you have to pick up your car—where is it?'

'By Blue Ridge Cove. I was spending the afternoon there, taking some time out to get to know the area.'

'That's more or less on my way home. I'll give you a lift.'

The unexpected offer threw her off balance. 'I don't want to put you out...'

'You won't. Let's go, shall we?' Briskly, without giving her any more chance to discuss the matter, he led the way down to the car park and across to a gleaming midnight blue saloon.

He appeared to be in a hurry, and as soon as she was settled in the luxuriously upholstered seat beside him, he started the engine and drove smoothly out onto the main highway.

'You said that you were getting to know the area... you're new to Cornwall, then?' he queried as they left the town and headed towards the cove. He glanced at her obliquely, and when she nodded, he asked, 'Where have you come from?'

'London. I've lived there for a number of years, because that's where I did most of my medical training, but I decided that I wanted a change, the chance to come and live by the coast for a while and breathe in some fresh sea air.'

Abby wasn't going to tell him that part of her reasoning in coming here was that she had hoped to escape from her ex-boyfriend. She was determined to make a new start, free from the worries of Richard's persistent refusal to accept that the relationship was over.

'That's a big change,' he murmured. 'Have you left your family behind? Friends?'

'Friends, yes—I shall miss them. My brother lives down here, though, and my mother lives fairly nearby, in Devon, so I shall be able to see more of her than I did before.'

'And your father?'

She might have known that he would pick up on that omission. She was saddened, thinking about her father. 'He died some years ago,' she said quietly.

'I'm sorry.' He flicked her another brief glance. 'At least you'll have your brother close by.'

She shook her head. 'Unfortunately, I won't. He's working abroad for a few months, but he's letting me stay at his house in the meantime. It makes things easier for me, and Daniel will feel happier knowing that the house is being looked after while he's away.'

'Even so, you're taking a huge step, moving away from everything you've been used to. Choosing a coastal area when you've been used to city life is an immense change. You can't have come to that decision lightly.'

'I didn't, of course. I wanted to study emergency medicine, and the Roseland has a good reputation as a teaching hospital.'

His blue-grey eyes searched her face. 'So do a lot of others.'

She sensed that he was still doubtful of her logic, and that he was expecting her to say more, but she didn't want to go into her real reasons for moving down here. She wasn't ready to talk to anyone about the worries she had back in London, least of all to Jordan Blakesley.

If he knew that she was afraid of a man who had become too possessive, too demanding, his opinion of her would take a nosedive. He would probably dismiss her as incredibly weak and lacking in backbone. How could he possibly comprehend the way that Richard had begun to exert an insidious hold on her, refusing to let her live her life as a free agent? She could barely understand it herself.

By now, they had arrived at the clifftop where her car was parked. Drawing up alongside it, Jordan cut the engine and let his gaze narrow on her. 'Life down here is vastly different from that in the City, but if you're expecting it to be easier, you're in for a disappointment. In the summer months we're inundated with visitors to the area and the hospital takes the strain.'

'Yes, I guessed that.'

'Are you sure? You'll be under pressure a lot of the time.'

'I appreciate that, I'm not afraid of hard work.'

'There will be no time for indecision and wallowing in uncertainty.'

Her mouth quirked in a wry grimace. 'I'll try to bear that in mind,' she murmured. She guessed his opinion of her wasn't great. No matter that she had managed to save a man's life this afternoon, he believed that she had been uncertain and anxious, and he wasn't a man to tolerate shortcomings in his colleagues.

'Good. I'll expect to see you tomorrow, bright and early, then. Just remember,' he added on a warning note, 'that if you do make any mistakes, I want to know about them straight away, so that they can be put right.'

'I understand that.'

'I hope that you do.'

She hunted for her car keys in her bag, and then slid out of the passenger seat. 'I must go. Thanks for the lift.'

'You're welcome.' He watched her walk to her car, waiting until she had unlocked it and started up the engine. Then he drove away.

Abby's glance followed him, her emotions a chaotic jumble of uncertainty and apprehension. The man was an enigma and, not for the first time that day, she wondered just what she was letting herself in for.

CHAPTER TWO

'WHERE are you going? Are you going to work?' A small voice sounded by Abby's side as she left the house to go to her car the next morning, and she looked down to see a young girl, around four years old, her golden curls gleaming in the morning sunshine.

'Hello,' Abby said. 'Yes, I am.' She smiled at the little girl. 'You must be Chloe—do you live next door?' Abby's next-door neighbour, Jessica, was her brother's girlfriend. She had met the woman once, when her brother had introduced them, but on the various occasions when she had seen her since, Chloe had been at nursery school or playing at a friend's house, and this was the first time that she had seen her to talk to her.

'Yes. I live with my mummy.'

'Where is your mummy?' Abby asked thoughtfully. She was concerned, all at once. What was the child doing out here on her own on the shared drive? Luckily, the front gates were shut, and their latches were probably too stiff for the child to manage by herself, but there was always the possibility that she might try to climb over them.

'She's not very well.'

'Isn't she?' Abby frowned. 'What's wrong with her, do you know?'

Chloe shrugged her shoulders, and Abby glanced

over at her neighbour's house and saw that the front
door was open.

'Did you open the door?' she asked.

Chloe nodded, pleased with herself. 'I got a stool
and opened it,' she confided. 'I'm big now.'

'Yes, you are, aren't you? I can see that.' Taking
the child's hand, she said, 'Let's go and see if we can
find your mother, shall we?' Abby led her towards
the house, just as Jessica appeared at the door, looking frantic.

'Oh, there she is. Thank heaven. I was so worried.'

'It's all right, Jessica. She's safe.' Abby briefly
scanned her neighbour's face and noted the dark shadows beneath her eyes, which emphasised the paleness
of her features. Her skin had a faintly sallow appearance, and her dark hair tumbled to her shoulders in
straggly waves. 'Are you OK? Chloe said that you
were ill.'

'I was being sick.' Jessica pulled a face. 'Some
kind of stomach bug, I expect. I thought Chloe was
still asleep, but she must have got out of bed and
come downstairs while I was in the bathroom.' She
frowned. 'I never imagined she could get out of the
house by herself.' She opened the door wider. 'Come
on in.'

Abby went into the house. 'Perhaps you need to
have a bolt fitted,' she suggested, inspecting the door-
frame. 'I'm surprised that you don't have one already.'

Jessica grimaced. 'There was one once.' She
rubbed her stomach, clearly still feeling unwell. 'It
obviously wasn't a very good one, because it was
damaged when my ex-husband came around one
night and tried to force his way in. I've been meaning

to get it fixed, but with going out to work and not feeling too well lately, and one thing and another, I haven't had the time.'

Abby frowned. It sounded as though Jessica's ex-husband was a belligerent character. No wonder Jessica looked tired and washed-out if that was the kind of problem she was experiencing on a day-to-day basis. No one could live with that kind of strain for any length of time without it affecting her health, especially now that Daniel was away. 'Isn't that a bit worrying?' she murmured. 'No wonder my brother wanted me to keep an eye on you.'

'Did he say that? Daniel's a lovely man.' Jessica gave a faint smile. 'He's so thoughtful and kind... nothing at all like Colin, my ex.' They walked through to the kitchen and she sighed wearily and sank down onto a wooden chair.

'Is Colin likely to try to do the same thing again?' Abby asked.

'He might do, although the police have warned him to stay away. They gave me a panic alarm so that I could contact them any time I needed help. I'll get the bolt sorted out today. I don't want Chloe to wander off again.'

'Are you going to be all right looking after her if you're not feeling well?' Even though she was conscious that she ought to be setting out on her journey to work, Abby was worried about leaving her neighbour to cope on her own, and she felt even more responsible as she was her brother's girlfriend.

'I'll manage, thanks.' She ran a hand through her hair. 'I'll drop her off at nursery school and go and see the doctor. I shan't go into work today.'

'What about your family? Are your parents able to help out?'

Jessica shook her head. 'We had a big falling out when I married Colin. They didn't like him and they warned me against marrying him, but I went ahead anyway, and they were angry with me. I haven't had much contact with them over the last few years. At first I was loyal to Colin, and later I was too proud to admit that they had been right all along. It got more difficult to get in touch as time went on.'

'I'm sorry.' That seemed so sad to Abby, to be isolated from your family when they were still around, but there was no time for her to talk about it now, and Jessica was looking poorly again.

Abby said quickly, 'Look, you don't look at all well. I'll have a word with Mrs Matthews next door, shall I? She seems nice and friendly, and she's on her own. She'll probably be glad to help out if you're in a fix.'

Jessica was probably feeling too ill to disagree, because she bent over as though she was in some pain. Abby stayed with her long enough to see that she wasn't about to collapse, and then hurried away to find her other neighbour.

Mrs Matthews's eyes widened when Abby explained the situation a minute or so later. In her sixties, she was a widow, and she generally kept herself to herself, although she was friendly whenever Abby spoke to her.

'Of course I'll go round there right away and help out. You get yourself off to work, love. They'll be all right with me. Don't you worry.'

Relieved that she had resolved the situation in part, Abby got in her car and set off for work. After all these delays, she was certain that she was going to be late, and she was sure that Jordan wouldn't take kindly to that.

She had half hoped he would be too busy attending to a patient to notice her arrival when she finally hurried into the accident and emergency department, but she was out of luck.

'So you're here at last, Dr Curtis,' he said tersely, subjecting her to a laser-eyed scrutiny. 'I would have expected you to at least make an effort to be here on time on your first day.'

'I'm sorry I'm late,' she said. 'I would have been on time, but my neighbour—'

'Please, don't give me any excuses,' Jordan said crisply. 'I don't want to hear them, and I'm sure the patients don't either. You'll find the first one waiting for you in cubicle three.'

'I—I'll go and deal with it now. Right away.' She backed away from him, feeling flustered and out of sorts, then turned and headed for the cubicle. He could have at least let her explain.

As the day wore on, she settled uneasily into her role as senior house officer. The summer season was on them and, as well as the usual number of local people who attended A and E because of traffic accidents or work-related injuries, there were many holidaymakers who found themselves in trouble of one sort or another.

Abby did her best to stay calm and clear-thinking, and deal with everything that came her way, and after a while she began to feel that she was coping reasonably well. Then a child was brought in, suffering from flu-like symptoms, with muscle and joint pains.

The boy was ten years old, and complained of a

headache. 'He has a fever,' the nurse said quietly, and Abby nodded acknowledgement.

She smiled reassuringly at him, and said gently, 'I just need to examine you, Fraser. Can you tell me where it hurts most?'

'My knees,' he said, with a hint of breathlessness. 'I hurt everywhere, but my knees are the worst. My chest hurts as well.'

'OK. Let's take a look at you.' She ran the stethoscope over his chest and heard a faint irregularity of the heartbeat. 'We'll do an ECG,' she told the nurse in an undertone. 'There may be some inflammation around the heart that's causing his breathlessness.'

The boy's knee joints were swollen, she discovered. Frowning a little, she tried to work out what it was that was causing Fraser's symptoms. 'Let's do blood tests as well to see if there's an infection.'

Turning to his mother, she said, 'We're going to do tests to find out what could be causing his illness. As soon as we have the results, we'll be able to consider our treatment options. In the meantime, we'll need to admit him for observation.'

Jordan appeared at her side just then, and indicated that he wanted to talk to her privately. She wondered how long he had been watching her. Throughout the day, she had been conscious of him in the background, and she was sure he was keeping an eagle eye on her progress. The last thing she wanted to do was to let him know that she was floundering, but she didn't know quite how she could avoid it.

'Are you having trouble making a diagnosis?' he asked softly, when they had retreated outside the cubicle, leaving the boy with his mother.

'It isn't anything I've come across before,' she admitted. 'I think it may be an infection of some kind, especially if it's affecting his heart in some way, as well as his joints.'

'May I take a look?' he enquired, and she agreed readily enough.

Jordan introduced himself to the boy and his mother, and made a careful examination, just as Abby had already done. 'On holiday, are you?' he asked Fraser, and the boy nodded.

'We came here about ten days ago,' his mother said.

Jordan smiled. 'It's beautiful around here, isn't it?' He glanced back at the boy, and said lightly, 'Have you been taking the coastal walks hereabouts, or do you think you might have been overdoing the football?'

'No football,' Fraser answered, struggling a little for breath, 'but we've done lots of walking.'

Jordan gently examined the boy's calves. 'Did you keep to the paths, or have you sometimes wandered through the fields?'

The boy looked puzzled, and said anxiously, 'Both. Did I do something wrong?'

'Nothing at all,' Jordan answered cheerfully. 'I like to take the coastal walks myself. There are some lovely views over the bay.' He turned to Abby and pointed out a slightly reddened area on the boy's calf. 'Do you see that?' he asked.

She had missed it. It was fairly insignificant, and it wasn't something that she would have paid much heed to under normal circumstances. Now, though, she sent Jordan a questioning look.

'What is it?'

'A tick bite, most likely. Sometimes they're quite

pronounced, but if this happened a few days ago the area around the bite might have settled down a bit.' He showed the child the reddened patch and said quietly, 'I think you might have been bitten by a tick when you were on one of your walks. They're usually found on sheep or deer, but walkers can suffer from their bites occasionally. They can pass on an infection called Lyme disease, which may lead to symptoms like yours. We'll know for certain when the test results come through.'

'What does it mean?' Fraser's mother asked. 'Can you treat it?'

'We can. If it is Lyme disease, we'll start him off on a ten-day course of antibiotics, and he'll need anti-inflammatory drugs to bring down the swelling and help relieve the pain. We'll most likely put him on corticosteroids for a while, too.'

He smiled once again at Fraser and moved away from the bedside. 'We'll sort you out,' he said. 'Don't worry.'

The mother followed Jordan and said in a low voice, 'Will he be cured? I mean, will there be any after-effects, any permanent damage to his joints?'

'There shouldn't be. It may take a few weeks for him to be fully well, but he should be fine before too long. He'll need to rest in the meantime.'

Looking a little more reassured, the woman went back to her son.

Away from the cubicle, Abby bit her lip. 'I've never come across that before. Can you be certain that's what it is?'

He gave a crooked smile, one that added a roguish attractiveness to his features. 'You're a city girl,' he said bluntly. 'You're not likely to be familiar with it.

In any case, the tests will take away any element of guesswork. Lyme disease is known mostly in the US, but it's also a problem in Europe and part of our own southern heathlands. You were right to admit him. He'll need support over the next few days, especially if his heart is involved, but he should make a full recovery.'

'I'm glad. He looks so ill and wretched just now, poor boy.'

He slanted her a narrowed glance. 'If you're not sure about anything, just ask.' His tone was brisk. 'You can't be expected to know everything, and it doesn't reflect badly on you if you ask for a second opinion.'

'I'll remember that.'

'I hope you will.'

He moved away then, to attend to another patient, and she was left thinking that perhaps he wasn't as bad as her first impression of him had led her to believe. He could be acerbic at times, but at least he hadn't had a go at her in front of the patients.

There was no time to dwell on things, though. More patients needed her attention and she made an effort to pull her mind back to her work. Whatever she did, she was going to be watched, but maybe in time he would realise that she was a capable doctor and he would learn to trust her.

The day wore on, and at mid-afternoon, when she was thinking she could do with a break and a cup of coffee, Sarah, the nurse who had been working with her said, 'There's a phone call for you, Abby.' She laid the receiver down on the desk and walked over to where Abby was signing off some charts.

Abby frowned. 'Who is it?' She couldn't think of

anyone who would be ringing her up at work. Her mother hardly ever called during working hours, not wanting to interrupt her in case she was busy.

Sarah gave a grimace. 'I don't know, he didn't say. He just said he wanted to talk to Dr Abby Curtis.' She lowered her voice and confided, 'I wouldn't mind getting his number, though. He sounded wonderful. His voice is really deep and sexy.' Her blue eyes crinkled at the corners. 'If you don't want him, just pass him my way, would you? I'm footloose and fancy-free.'

Abby chuckled. 'Well, I will, if it's my brother. I can certainly pass him on to you...but I have to warn you, you might have to wait a while to meet up with him. He's in South America right now, and he's not due back for several months.'

Sarah pulled a rueful face. 'Isn't that just my luck?' she said, turning away to find Jordan waiting for her.

He must have heard their conversation, but his expression revealed no hint of his thoughts. 'Would you suture a gashed hand for me in cubicle four?' he asked.

Sarah nodded. 'Will do.'

Jordan went to follow up on a patient of his own, and Abby walked over to the phone on the other side of the room.

In fact, she didn't think Daniel would be ringing her at the hospital. If he wanted to get in touch, he would be far more likely to use a cheaper method of communication, like e-mail or fax, with perhaps a more private call home once a month.

The phone was housed in a Plexiglas booth, which provided a modicum of privacy. Abby picked up the receiver and said, 'Hello.'

There was no answer, just a silence, and she repeated, 'Hello, this is Abby Curtis. Who is it…who wants to speak to me?' Again there was silence, and after a moment the phone cut to the dialling tone.

Abby frowned. That was odd. She waited a moment, still holding the receiver and wondering what had happened. Perhaps the caller had been inadvertently cut off and would ring back. She replaced the receiver and waited, but nothing happened.

The more she thought about it, the more she wondered who the mystery caller could have been. She didn't know that many men who had deep, sexy voices, and the only one to spring to mind was the last person she would have expected to hear from.

Surely Richard couldn't have tracked her down? How could he have found out where she was? Unless someone had unwittingly told him…

Quickly, she dialled her mother's number and asked the question that was burning into her mind.

'Do you think there's any way that he could have found out where I am? You haven't said anything to him, have you? He hasn't phoned you?'

Her mother was calm and unruffled. 'You know I wouldn't have told him anything, Abby. I know how important it is to you that you get away from him. I always suspected that there was something strange about him, and I didn't want him anywhere near you once I got to know him better. I thought his obsession with you was unnatural.'

'I'm sorry. I was just afraid that you might have let something slip, without meaning to.'

'I didn't. I can't think how he could have found you so soon—and, anyway, you don't know for sure that it was him, do you? The caller could have realised that he had made a mistake and that it was a different Abby Curtis he was looking for—someone older perhaps, and that's why he rang off without speaking. He was probably embarrassed. Or it might have been that the nurse heard him wrong and he had asked for someone with a similar-sounding name.'

Abby might have known her mother would react like that. She was a sensible woman, whose reasoning was nearly always straightforward.

'You're probably right. I expect I'm making a fuss about nothing.' Abby talked to her mother for a minute or two longer, then said goodbye and hung up.

Her mood was pensive, though. Was she simply imagining things? No matter how Abby tried to brush it off, the thought niggled that the caller might have been Richard. Given that she had told him she didn't want anything more to do with him, he might well have been messing about, playing silly games with her.

It was a sad state of affairs, because their relationship had been good to begin with, she recalled. Richard had been sexy, appealing, persuasive, and she had found herself falling for him over the weeks that had passed.

It had only been later that she had realised there was another side to him, a part of his nature that needed to be in control, to take over, to have everything his way. That was when she had tried to break off the relationship, but her retreat had only made him more possessive, more argumentative, and when the split had finally come it had been fraught with tension. It had been worrying when he had accused her of seeing other men, falsely as it happened, and he had become steadily more resentful and threatening.

'We belong together,' he'd said, in a way that chilled her to the bone. 'If you ever try to leave me, you'll regret it. I won't let you go, and I'll not let any other man come near you.'

And now here she was, several months later, wondering whether even now it was still not finished with.

'Do you think you could go and dream about your love life in your own time?' Jordan's voice cut tersely across her thoughts. 'We're running an emergency department here, not a sweethearts' convention.'

'I wasn't… I mean…I was just called to the phone, that's all. I wasn't letting it interfere with my work.'

'Weren't you? While you were lost in fantasyland, patients have been lining up to be seen. If you can't keep your mind on the job, you shouldn't be here at all.'

'I'm allowed to take a break,' she said, her green eyes flashing him a cool challenge. 'Just because I choose to take it in a phone booth instead of the doctors' lounge doesn't make it any less valid, and I'm still around and ready if a major emergency comes in.'

'If you say so,' he threw back drily. 'Looking at you, some might have doubted that.' He thrust a chart into her hand. 'The woman in cubicle two has a possible migraine. She, at least, has a reasonable excuse for having a muzzy head.'

Abby took the chart without another word and went to examine the woman. Insufferable man. What was his problem? Did he think it was his life's work to provoke his colleagues, or was it just her that he had it in for? She had only met him the previous day and already she was having to bite her tongue for fear of landing herself out of a job.

Whatever had made her think being part of his team was a rung up the professional ladder? She might as well have tried cosying up to a snarling tiger.

CHAPTER THREE

JESSICA was still not feeling too well when Abby returned home that evening.

'Did you go and see the doctor?' Abby asked, going into the kitchen of the house next door. Jessica nodded. She still had very little colour and looked as though she was on the verge of collapse.

'He said it was probably a virus of some sort, but he gave me something to settle my stomach and told me to rest.' She gave a wry smile. 'That'll be the day—who can rest with a four-year-old running around? Actually, though, I don't feel as sick as I did this morning. Just this awful tiredness.'

'I can watch Chloe for you for an hour or two if you want to go and lie down,' Abby offered. 'You look as though you could do with a break.' She filled a kettle with water and set about making her neighbour a hot drink. 'If you've not eaten much today, perhaps you could try a little soup. I'll make some for you, shall I?'

'You're an angel. Thanks, though I'm not really hungry.' Jessica ran a hand wearily through her dark hair. 'You and Mrs Matthews have been so good to me today. Corinne took Chloe to nursery school and brought her home for me. I feel really bad about putting on you both like this.'

'Nonsense. I'm sure we both want to do what we can for you. It's not easy when you're feeling ill and you've a child to care for. As soon as you've eaten something, you should go and rest for a while. Doctor's orders!'

'Bless you,' Jessica said, closing her eyes for a moment as though her eyelids were weighted down. 'If you're adamant about it, I think I will. Chloe certainly seems to have taken to you.'

'She'll be fine with me. Don't you worry. I'll bring her back later and help get her ready for bed, if you like.'

'Thanks.'

Abby waited while Jessica managed some of the soup, and then settled her into bed.

Chloe was perfectly happy to come and make pink play dough in Abby's kitchen, and she used biscuit cutters to make shapes out of it while Abby got on with tackling a few chores.

'Dan'el writed a letter to my mummy,' Chloe volunteered, holding up a squidgy heart shape for Abby to admire. 'There was kisses on it.'

'That must have been nice for her,' Abby commented with a smile. There had been a letter from him among her own post when she had arrived home.

'Mmm. I think she liked it,' the child agreed. 'But Mummy's eyes was wet. She said she had a cold.'

Poor Jessica. Abby could imagine how wretched she must be feeling right now, both physically and mentally, with her family keeping their distance and the man she had come to rely on half the world away. And that was without trouble from her ex-husband to give her grief.

Over the next few weeks, Abby had problems of her own to contend with at the hospital, and she was on edge a lot of the time, trying to steer a steady course through the minefield of working with Jordan.

If he thought she was the slightest bit hesitant, he would query her decisions and make her account for every test that she ordered. So far, she had managed to keep on top of things, but it hadn't been easy.

Late one afternoon, she stopped by the desk to sign some forms for the laboratory and found herself stifling a yawn. She had been run off her feet for most of the day, and the thought of going home and soaking in a relaxing bath was uppermost in her mind.

Unhappily for her, Jordan chose that moment to sweep by, and pounced with deadly accuracy. 'Are we keeping you up, Abby?' he enquired in a low drawl.

She gazed up at him blankly for a moment.

His blue-grey eyes slanted down over her slender figure, noting the slight tilt of her shoulders and the negligent way she stood, one leg pressed up against the wooden front of the desk, the other foot eased out of her shoe while she rubbed her aching ankle against the calf of her other leg. She was suddenly aware of the narrow fit of her skirt, and the way her cotton top drifted upwards over her rib cage as she raised a hand to cover her mouth.

Too late, she tried to change the yawn into a cough, and his mouth twisted sardonically.

'Nice try,' he muttered drily, 'but totally unconvincing. Maybe you should tell your boyfriend to go home earlier so that you can get some sleep.'

The unfairness of it made her open her mouth in protest, but he had already moved on, striding towards the light box where he stopped to view a set of X-rays and offered an opinion to the registrar who was frowning at them in worried indecision.

It wasn't as though there was a scrap of truth in his accusation, Abby thought resentfully. She had stayed on last night after her shift should have ended to follow up on a patient that she had been admitting, and as a consequence she had only managed a couple of hours' sleep before coming into work this morning.

Why was it that she always seemed to get the sharp end of his tongue, while the rest of her colleagues escaped with samples of his dry wit?

It was so unfair, but she wasn't going to demean herself by explaining what had really happened, especially when he was deep in conversation with his registrar.

He crossed her path again when she was about to get in her car to drive home a couple of hours later.

'Finished for the day?' he enquired softly.

'I have,' she said, flicking a frosty glance in his direction. 'Any objections?'

She regretted the words as soon as she had said them. Junior doctors simply didn't talk to consultants like that—not if they wanted to get on. But it was out now, and he was giving her a brooding stare through thick, dark lashes, his eyes half-closed.

'None at all. Enjoy your evening,' he said.

It wasn't what she had expected and it threw her off balance. She sent him a wary glance. 'I will.'

She drove home and tried to shake the image of his sculpted features from her mind. He was there to vex and challenge her throughout her working day and she refused to let him disturb her off-duty time as well.

It wasn't so easy to dismiss him from her thoughts,

though, and she tried to forget about him by spending the evening with Jessica and Corinne Matthews in Jessica's garden. They sat out on the patio and talked quietly, sipping at glasses of chilled wine until it began to get dark. Then they decided to turn in for the night and each went back to her own home.

Abby was tired, and when she finally lay down in bed, she fell asleep straight away.

She didn't know what it was that woke her. One minute she was deep in slumber, the next she was sitting up in bed and staring around at the night shadows in confusion. The clock on her bedside table read a quarter to four, and she thought she caught a faint beam of light arcing through her bedroom curtains.

It was probably just moonlight, but for some reason her heart was pounding heavily. Then she heard a sound, like the click of a gate, and she suddenly felt fearful for Jessica and Chloe next door. Was Jessica's ex-husband on the prowl?

She slid her feet into soft mules and pulled her fleecy wrap around herself, while she tried to decide what she should do. Jessica might need some help, and Abby was determined to protect her and Chloe from any untoward happenings.

She crept down the stairs, thankful that the dim glow from the lamp she had left on in the hall lit her way. Going out through the back door of the house, she headed for Jessica's kitchen door. It was locked, but as she looked up, Abbey could see that the bathroom window was open.

Just then, the kitchen light came on, and Abby heard Chloe's small voice. 'Daddy here, Mummy?' she was asking.

Jessica's answer was muted, and Abby tapped on

the kitchen door and said in an urgent low voice, 'Jess—it's Abby. Can I come in?'

Abby heard the slide of a bolt and then Jessica opened the door. She was white-faced and her hands shook a little, but Abby could see that she was trying to appear calm for Chloe's sake.

'Me have lem'nade, Mummy?'

'No, Chloe. Not now.'

Abby went into the kitchen and shut the door behind her. 'I thought I heard something and I came to see if you were all right.'

Jessica nodded, and said in an undertone, 'I thought I heard someone prowling around outside, and got up to take a look. Then Chloe said she saw someone in her room, but she might have been dreaming.'

Abby looked at her in alarm. 'Have you checked the house?'

'Yes. There's no one here now, but the bathroom window has been forced open.' She frowned. 'I'll have to get that fixed as soon as I can. Perhaps I can block it up some way, just for tonight.'

'Why I not have lem'nade?' Chloe asked, rubbing her eyes.

'It's not good for you at this time of night. I'll make you a milk drink instead. You go and curl up on the settee and I'll bring it to you.'

Jessica settled her daughter, then fetched a saucepan from the cupboard and set about making hot chocolate.

She was trembling still, and Abby said quietly, 'I'll do that. You sit down. You look a bit wobbly on your feet.' She went to the hob and watched the milk heat in the pan, then poured it into mugs and stirred the chocolate thoughtfully. 'Do you think it was Colin?'

'I don't know. It might have been, but with him, trouble usually starts when he's had too much drink. He's not usually one to creep about.' She shivered and wrapped her arms around herself. 'Unless he's trying out some new way to upset me…I suppose you must think I'm feeble to let him get to me this way?'

Abby shook her head. 'No, I don't think that at all. I know what it's like to deal with someone who's unstable. I knew a man in London who could be menacing if he didn't get his own way. He was possessive and determined to have me as his girl friend. I even had to change my phone number because of him. I tried talking to him, reasoning with him, but nothing worked, and in the end I left. It was too wearing on my nerves to have to keep on dealing with him.'

'I think it's a bit like that with Colin. He can't bear to think that I don't want him any more. That's why he keeps coming back.'

'Have you called the police about tonight's break-in?'

Jessica shook her head. 'There doesn't seem to be much point. Whoever it was has gone now, and it would only upset Chloe to have police all over the place. Perhaps I'll tell them in the morning, when she's at nursery.'

'I suppose you're right.' Abby looked at Jessica's pale face and said, 'Shall I stay here with you for the rest of the night?'

'Would you? I must admit I'm feeling really wound up about all this. It's frightening to think that someone's been creeping about my house.'

'I would feel exactly the same.' Abby gave her a hug. 'We'll all feel safer if we stay together.'

She doubted that either of them would get much

sleep after that, but at least Chloe didn't appear to be too upset by the incident. They took the little girl up to bed a few minutes later, and she looked out of her bedroom window to satisfy herself that all was well before she climbed into bed. Then she got up again and said sleepily, 'Me go in Mummy's bed?'

'All right.' Jessica hugged her daughter close, and Abby settled down for what was left of the night in Chloe's room. When Jessica woke her in the morning, in time to get ready for work, she felt as though she had only just fallen asleep.

In the A and E department, Jordan was his usual energetic, breezy self, and Abby looked at him sourly through bleary eyes as the morning progressed. How did he manage to be so full of life, with such endless vitality? If he said as much as one small thing to her about looking tired she would not be responsible for her actions. As it was, she was still feeling anxious about the events of the night before, and her mood was fractious.

Chloe had bounced downstairs to breakfast as happily as ever, and had seemed not to be affected by what had gone on, except that when she had been biting on a slice of buttery toast she had said curiously, 'Dat man still in your house, Abby?'

Abby had blinked. 'What man, sweetheart?'

Chloe had shrugged awkwardly and had then looked at her with a touch of uncertainty as though she had felt she might have said something wrong. 'I sawed him.'

'When did you see him, Chloe?'

'In the dark. I looked out my window.' Then Chloe had stopped speaking, and had resolutely refused to answer any more questions, no matter how tentatively they had been put to her.

Abby had been worried. She had made a quick check of the house, realising too late that she had left the back door unlocked in her haste last night, but there had been no sign of anything untoward, nothing appeared to be missing, and she had begun to wonder whether Chloe had imagined it.

Then, as she had been preparing to set off for work, she had discovered the imprint of a man's shoe in the shrubbery outside her patio doors. The sight of it had sent a chill through her whole body.

Perhaps Jordan recognised that she was out of sorts and not to be messed with, because he gave her a sideways glance as she snatched up a patient's case file from the desk and briskly scanned it, but he said nothing.

'I've had Mr Stevens' test results back from the lab,' Sarah said, coming up behind her, and Abby jumped as though she had been scalded.

Recovering, she said quietly, 'Thanks, Sarah. I'll let him know.'

They were busy in the department, and she didn't have time to stop and dwell on things, but in the late afternoon, when they had finished dealing with a nasty road traffic accident, she was having a quick cup of coffee when Sarah called her to her next patient.

'She's been brought in by a neighbour,' Sarah said. 'The neighbour thinks she's been knocked about by her boyfriend—there's a history of injuries over the past three years, but the woman isn't admitting to anything. She has a fever and she looks very poorly.

She's complaining of severe headache and pain in and above the eye. I've put her in cubicle five.'

'OK, I'll take a look at her right away.'

Abby was shocked by the woman's facial injuries, but she didn't let her see that she was affected. Instead, she murmured sympathetically, 'That looks as though it must be really hurting, Rhea. How did it happen?'

'I tripped and banged my face on a door,' the woman answered. She was aged around thirty, and her cheekbone and eye socket were swollen. There was also a split in the skin, which looked as though it had started healing but infection had set in. She looked ill.

'This must have happened a few days ago,' Abby murmured, inspecting the wound. 'It looks as though the cheek has become infected…it must be very tender. Didn't you go and see your doctor for treatment?'

'No, I…I didn't want to bother him. I thought it would clear up on its own.'

'Are you having any problems with your vision?'

'Yes, things are a bit blurred.'

'All right, Rhea. You rest there, while I go and consult with a colleague. We're going to have to admit you, so that we can clear up the infection as quickly as possible. It's possible that there's a small clot forming at the back of the eye, which is building up the pressure there and causing your visual disturbance, so we need to deal with that as well. I'll leave you with the nurse, so that she can take a swab. That will help us to identify the bacterium causing the infection.'

She left the cubicle and went to find Jordan. He

was with a patient, but he came to talk to her as soon as she asked, and she quickly told him about Rhea.

'I think I need to start her on antibiotics straight away, and I'm organising a scan. Should I give her anticoagulants? I'm pretty sure that she has a thrombosis as a result of the infection, and her sight is already being affected.'

'Yes, that's the best course of action. If we don't act quickly she could lose her sight altogether. It's not something that we come across often these days—mostly infections are cleared up by antibiotics before they can get this far, but she probably left it because she didn't want to let anyone see what had happened.'

'She has a history of unexplained injuries,' Abby said. 'It sounds as though she's suffering from domestic violence. Can't we do something to make sure that this doesn't happen again? Can't we involve the police?'

'We can't do anything unless she agrees to it. The police won't be able to bring a prosecution if she refuses to lay a charge.'

'It doesn't feel right to do nothing at all. How long can she go on being battered like this? There must be something we can do.'

'Give her the name of a local refuge and ask her if you can get in touch with the people running it. They'll do the rest.'

'It doesn't seem to be enough.'

'It's all you can do. You can't take on everyone's problems, Abby. We're here to patch them up, that's all.'

'It makes me feel so angry, so helpless.'

'It makes any decent person feel that way, but getting angry won't stop it. You have to move on, and deal with the rest of your patients.'

He turned away then, and went back to the man he was treating, leaving Abby to stand there and quietly fume for a while. Why did people treat each other this way? Hadn't Jessica suffered in a similar fashion? Her ex had been violent, but at least she had gone to the police and they were doing what they could to help her.

It all made Abby dwell on her own situation. That was not quite so clear, was it? Who was it that had gone into her house last night? Would she ever feel safe again, knowing that there was a prowler around?

Abby went to organise medication for Rhea, and arrange for her admission, and when she had done that she decided to ring Jessica. She should be home from work by now, and she wanted to make sure that she was safe.

Jessica was a part-time secretary for a local solicitor, and the hours fitted in fairly well with Chloe's nursery school, though she was finding it a bit of a strain these days. She was still feeling under the weather, with bouts of sickness every now and again.

'How are things? Have there been any more problems?' Abby asked.

'Everything appears to be OK,' Jessica answered. 'I told the police that we thought someone was hanging around, and that he had been in the house, but they said there wasn't much they could do, since nothing had been taken. I showed them the broken window catch, and they gave me an incident number.'

'Perhaps he was frightened away by something. Maybe he heard a car and thought someone was coming home. Anyway, I'm glad you told the police,'

Abby said. 'Look, I have to get back to work now, but I should be back home in just over an hour. We'll talk then.'

She rang off a moment or two later, and when Sarah stopped to ask if she was OK, she said, 'Yes, I'm fine. Why?'

'Oh, you seemed a bit upset earlier... When you came in to work, you weren't your usual self, and then there was the woman with the facial injury. Then, just now, on the phone, I couldn't help noticing that you looked worried about something. I'm not meaning to interfere—I just wanted you to know that if you wanted to talk anything through, I'm here.'

Abby gave her a quick smile. 'Thanks, Sarah. I'm OK, really. I was just phoning a friend who's had a spot of bother. Actually, she works for a solicitor, so you'd think she would get better advice from him than from me, but I needed to ring her all the same.'

'Is he any good...the solicitor?' Sarah asked. 'I want to sell my house, but I don't want to use a firm who will spin things out and then charge me a fortune. I've found the ideal flat and I was hoping that I could move fairly quickly.'

'Jessica said he's very good. He handled her divorce and his partner saw to the sale of her house. I can give you his number if you like—it's in my bag. I kept it, because I shall need to find a place of my own when my brother gets back.'

'Thanks.'

Abby went to her locker and retrieved her bag, then rummaged in it for the number. 'Here you are.' She wrote it down on a scrap of paper and handed it to Sarah just as the fire alarm sounded.

They looked at each other in dismay. 'I thought I

smelled something in the air earlier,' Sarah said with a grimace. 'We'd better get going.'

It took several minutes to get everybody moved to a safe distance, and for a while it looked chaotic in the department as the walking wounded headed for the exits and the more seriously injured people were wheeled out of harm's way.

'My patient's gone into cardiac arrest,' Sarah said suddenly, and Abby hurried to assist.

'Somebody get me an oxygen cylinder and face mask,' she called out.

Sarah gave mouth-to-mouth resuscitation while they waited for the oxygen to arrive, and Abby did cardiac compressions, pressing down with the heel of one hand on top of the other to stimulate his heart into beating. 'Three, four, five. Pause. One, two, three, four, five, pause.'

'It's not working,' she said anxiously. 'There's still no response.'

'We'll try adrenaline.' Jordan appeared at Abby's side and injected the man, just as the all-clear bell sounded.

'I've found a pulse,' Abby said a moment later, relief in her voice.

'OK, let's get him inside, and get an ECG trace.'

Together, they wheeled the man back into A and E where they hooked him up to oxygen and obtained IV access.

'That was well done,' Jordan said, looking around at his team a minute or so later when the man's condition had been stabilised.

There was relief all round, and when someone asked where the fire had been, Jordan said drily, 'There was no fire. It was a fault with a boiler, apparently, that triggered the alarm. Just another of those episodes that keep us on our toes.'

Abby reflected that the siren had got them all jumping into action and wondered whether she ought to have an alarm fitted back at the house. She wasn't going to sleep easy while there was a chance that someone would try to gain access to her home. She would tell Daniel what she planned to do, but she knew that he wouldn't object. He was more likely to be concerned for herself and Jessica.

'Shouldn't you have gone off duty an hour ago?'

Abby jumped as Jordan's voice dragged her back to A and E. Flustered, she glanced down at the watch on her wrist. 'Yes, you're right. I should. I'll just finish writing up my notes and then I'll go.'

She spent a few minutes dealing with all the loose ends from the day's work, and then reached for her jacket and went out to the car park. How was she going to make her home safe against intruders for the coming night? If Jessica's ex-husband could break through a door bolt, what was going to be an effective deterrent?

She reached into her pocket for her keys and unlocked her car door. Should she offer to stay with Jessica tonight, to be there in case she was needed? But the man had gone to Abby's house after Jessica's, hadn't he? Perhaps it had been Abby he had been after all along.

She drove home along the winding coast road. It was a summer evening, but it had been a dull, cloudy day, and the sky was oppressive. The cliffs that she glimpsed in the distance looked looming and ominous, and the sea was crashing on to the rocks with demonic force. She shivered a little.

Abby parked her car in the garage. There was no one in when she knocked at Jessica's door, and Corinne came out to say, 'I think she's taken Chloe to a friend's house to stay the night. She wasn't feeling very well and she seemed to be a bit concerned when you were late getting back, and said something about staying there herself. Is everything all right?'

'Yes, though she's not been well for a while, has she? Thanks, Corinne.' Abby didn't tell her about last night's episode. Corinne had obviously not been disturbed in the night, and there was no sense in worrying her unduly. Abby was glad Jessica had sorted something out for tonight. She obviously was spooked enough to want to give herself some space.

Abby let herself into her brother's house and stared around at the walls. In the hall, in the kitchen, there was silence and emptiness. All at once, there seemed to be shadows everywhere and the house seemed cold. She drew her jacket around herself and hugged it to her.

The doorbell rang suddenly, and she froze. It sounded again, and she walked slowly back into the hall and saw the dark shape of a man's head and shoulders outlined against the opaque glass of the door. Pulling in a deep breath, she went to answer it. If she discovered that it was a stranger on the doorstep, she would send him away and lock the door. And if he resisted…

It was Jordan. Abby's relief was palpable, the tension seeping out of her in a long, harsh breath. She swallowed and made an effort to smile. She hoped he hadn't noticed anything amiss with her. He was giving her a strange look, and she didn't want to invite any questions just then.

'Hello. I didn't expect to see you here.' She frowned. 'How did you know where I lived?'

'I asked Sarah. You left your bag in the locker—apparently, when the fire alarm sounded, you shoved it back in, but forgot to lock the door. I said I would bring it to you, since you don't normally leave it at the hospital. Sarah thought you might need it, and it was on my way home.'

He held the bag out to her, and she stared at it uncomprehendingly for a moment. Then she recovered herself and took it from him. 'Thank you. I don't even remember pushing it back in there.'

'It's not surprising—you were distracted.' He gave her a searching look. 'May I come in?'

She glanced up at him quickly. 'Oh…yes, of course. Come in.' She stood back to allow him in, and then carefully shut the door. Glancing down, she saw a few letters that the postman must have delivered while she was out, and she scooped them up. There was a white postcard among them.

'I thought you would need your bag for your car keys,' Jordan said quietly, 'but from the looks of things you had them somewhere else.'

She blinked, then pushed her bag under her arm and felt in her pocket with her free hand. 'I must have absent-mindedly left them in my jacket,' she muttered, frowning. She hadn't given them a thought, and that showed how things were getting to her, didn't it? She ought to get a grip on herself.

'Would you like a cup of coffee?' she asked. 'I'll go and put the kettle on.'

'Thanks.' Jordan followed her along the passageway to the kitchen. 'Are you in trouble of some sort?' he asked bluntly, and she sent him a wide-eyed glance.

'What makes you say that?' she countered, playing for time. He was too observant, too persistent, for her liking. He was the same at work, and that was partly what made him such a good doctor. He delved and probed, and he didn't give up until he had sorted out a situation. He followed his instincts, and for the most part his instincts turned out to be right.

'You've been behaving oddly all day. Jumpy and a bit on edge, as though something's on your mind.'

'I'm fine. I had a restless night, that's all. Not enough sleep, I expect. These last few nights have been hot, haven't they? And now it looks as though we're in for a storm.'

His brows drew together, and he watched her put her bag down on the kitchen table, along with the letters. She snapped on the light to brighten the room and busied herself filling the kettle.

'I'll just make us a drink,' she said. 'I can make some toasted sandwiches, too, if you like. I'm starving—I didn't get a chance to get any lunch, with one thing and another. I don't suppose you did either.' She was talking quickly, anything to keep him from asking any more questions.

'I didn't. I'd like that, thank you.'

She washed her hands at the sink and then prepared slices of bread for the sandwich-maker. 'Ham and cheese?' she asked, and he nodded.

'That sounds great. Can I do anything to help?'

She shook her head. 'No, it's all right... I know where everything is. Sit down and take the weight off your feet.' He was long-limbed and exuded strength and vigour, and she couldn't think straight with him standing around. All the same, his presence in the room was somehow heartening.

He sat down at the table and looked around the

kitchen. It was all clean lines, with dove grey units offset by hints of soft blues and pale yellows in the crockery and gadgets that stood on the shelves and worktops.

Abby concentrated her attention on making the toasted sandwiches. She closed the lid on the machine and flicked the switch, then turned her attention to making the coffee. Jordan hadn't spoken for a minute or two, and she turned to glance at him.

He was looking down at the stack of letters on the table in front of him, and the card was uppermost. He frowned, and she wondered what he was reading.

'Is something wrong?'

'You tell me,' he said, pushing the card towards her. 'It's none of my business, but it probably explains a lot.'

She studied the card. It was in Jessica's handwriting.

Abby, I was so worried after what happened last night. I waited for you to come home, but when you were late I started to get anxious, especially being here on my own with Chloe. I'm going to stay with a friend overnight. I'm sorry to leave you in the house alone. Will you ring me at this number so that I know you're safe, too? Why don't you come over to us? Jane won't mind. Love, Jessica.

Jordan's deep voice broke in on her thoughts. 'I knew that something was on your mind. Why don't you tell me what's been going on?'

CHAPTER FOUR

'SO… COME on, out with it. What's been going on, Abby?'

Abby gave a shaky sigh. She wasn't going to be able to keep it to herself any longer, was she? Jordan wasn't going to let the matter drop. She had wanted to prove to him that she was confident and independent, but he was bound to find out the truth now and realise how vulnerable she really was. He hadn't had a great opinion of her to begin with, and now she would go down even more in his estimation.

She said flatly, 'Someone broke into the house next door while my neighbour was sleeping. I heard something and went to find out if she was all right, and it looks as though the intruder came into my house, too, while I wasn't there. Nothing was taken, though. Perhaps we disturbed him and he thought better of what he was planning to do. Anyway, he managed to give us the slip.'

Jordan's brows came together in a dark line. 'Are you sure nothing is missing?'

'I'm pretty sure. I had a quick look around this morning before work, but everything seems to be more or less in place.' She chewed at her lip. 'I suppose that's what makes it so sinister… We don't know what he was after.'

'Have you spoken to the police?'

'I haven't, but Jessica, my neighbour, did and she

was told that there's not very much the police can do about it.'

Jordan's features darkened. 'Why on earth didn't you tell me any of this before now?' He seemed angry all of a sudden, and she looked at him guardedly.

'I didn't see the need to tell anyone. I can handle it by myself.'

His expression was grim. 'You obviously can't. You've been on edge all day, and it was perfectly clear to me that something was wrong. You should have said something to me about it.'

'Why? What point would there have been? There's nothing you could do, and it's just something I have to deal with on my own.'

His jaw tightened. 'That's my point exactly. You shouldn't be dealing with something like this on your own. You're part of a team now, and if anything happens to upset you and interfere with the way you do your job, you should tell me so that I can support you. There's absolutely no reason for you to try to muddle through this alone. It's irresponsible of you.'

Her green eyes flashed a warning. 'I'm not irresponsible,' she shot back at him, incensed that he should make such an accusation.

'Of course you are, if you keep things like this to yourself. Having your house broken into is a worrying thing, and it's almost certain to prey on your mind and influence the way you behave. That in turn can affect your work. You're a doctor and the decisions you make can affect people's lives. If you're in any way distracted, you could put them at risk.'

Her brows arched. 'So I'm distracted now, am I?' She resented him having a go at her when she was the injured party and she'd done everything she could to cope with the situation. 'I'm perfectly capable of doing my work properly. I wouldn't dream of letting my private problems affect my patients' well-being.'

'You may not always have any choice. You're simply human, Abby, and that means that at times you may be tired and you may have anxieties. Either of those things can cause you to make mistakes. It's your responsibility to make sure that you seek help when you need it.'

'I don't recall making any mistakes.'

'Well, hopefully you didn't today, but there's always a first time. You shouldn't try to deal with something like this on your own.'

She didn't answer, wondering whether she could have handled the situation any differently than she had. She looked at him, her eyes troubled.

Jordan returned her gaze, then frowned suddenly and sniffed the air, looking around the kitchen. He said cautiously, 'Should the sandwich-maker be smoking that way?'

Startled, Abby followed his glance. 'Oh, heavens,' she muttered, rushing over and lifting the lid. Cautiously, she inspected the triangular sandwiches, gingerly testing them with her fingers. 'They're all right, I think,' she said, making a face. 'They're not burned, just what you might call…very well done.' She looked across the room at him, and he grinned unexpectedly.

'Well done sounds just fine to me.' He was still smiling, and Abby thought how different he looked when his face relaxed. He seemed younger, and the good-natured tilt to his mouth added an intriguing dimension to his already striking features.

She forced herself to concentrate and pushed a mug of coffee towards him. 'Help yourself to sugar.'

She slid the toasted sandwiches onto plates and sat down opposite him at the table.

'I suppose you're right,' she admitted eventually. 'Perhaps I should have told you what happened, but I thought it was something I needed to work out for myself.'

'I'm here to help. You need to feel safe in your own home, and perhaps it would be a start to think about getting some security systems in place.'

She nodded. 'I thought about getting an alarm fitted, but I'm not sure what else I can do.'

'You could have some security lights put up. The lights come on if somebody approaches the house, and that should help to put them off. I doubt if anyone up to no good wants to find themselves in a spotlight all of a sudden.' He bit into his sandwich and savoured it. 'This is good,' he murmured appreciatively. 'I didn't realise how hungry I was till now.'

'Me, too.' She nibbled at the toast.

'Are you going to join your neighbour—Jessica— at her friend's house?'

Abby thought about it for a moment, but then shook her head. 'I don't think so. I don't blame Jessica for going away. She isn't too well, and she has a four-year-old daughter to think about. She's also missing Daniel a great deal, but I don't think it's the answer for me. It would feel a bit like running away, and I'll only have to come back and face the situation again some time.'

'That's not an easy choice to make.' Surprisingly, his eyes held a tinge of respect for her decision.

'No…well, I'd rather deal with it sooner than later, otherwise it would only weigh on my mind.'

'Is there anyone in your family who could stay with you?'

She shook her head. 'My mother lives too far away, and I wouldn't want to worry her with this. She has a house near to the coast in Devon, near enough for me to visit at the weekend, but not close enough for day-to-day contact.'

'And your brother's away, you said. Is he the only one?'

'Yes, he is. He's working on a geological survey in South America, and he's not likely to be able to take a break for a month or so.'

She paused to eat her sandwich and found it surprisingly good. She tested the melted cheese on the tip of her tongue and then popped the last morsel into her mouth. Looking up, she saw that Jordan was watching her with a faintly bemused expression. She wondered if there was grease on her face, and to cover her confusion she reached for a paper serviette and dabbed at her mouth, then wiped her fingers clean.

'What happened to your father?' he asked. 'Do you mind talking about it?'

Abby shook her head. 'Not really. It was a long time ago, and my feelings are not so raw nowadays.' She grimaced. 'I was fourteen when he died…he left a big gap in my life. I thought the world of him. He had such a wonderful personality…everybody liked him. He would do anything for anybody.' She smiled, remembering, but after a moment her eyes clouded.

'We used to live about thirty miles from here, and he was doing a coastal walk one day when he saw a child fall from the cliff. He went to see what had happened to him and found that he had fallen onto a ledge, several feet below. He was injured and my father knew that he wouldn't be able to get him back up to the clifftop without help. The tide was coming in and he could see that the boy was frightened, so he called the emergency services and then went down to him and waited with him until help came. The sea was rising and he held the boy up out of the water until paramedics arrived.'

Jordan frowned. 'Did they manage to rescue the boy?'

'Yes. His worst injury was a fractured ankle, and he was suffering from cold and shock, but he came out of it all right in the end.'

'And your father? What happened to him?'

'It had been a big strain on him, holding the boy up until help came. The paramedics lifted the boy up first and then went to help my father, but by then he had been in the water for a long time and he was chilled to the bone. He was weakening by the minute, I think, and the waves were getting stronger. Somehow, he lost his footing and collapsed. They managed to get to him, but he died of a heart attack in hospital later that night.'

'I'm so sorry.' Jordan's expression was bleak. 'That must have been dreadful for all of you.'

'It was. We moved away from the area after that, and I didn't want to come back for a long time. I didn't want to be reminded of what had happened. I suppose the only good thing that came out of it was that it fuelled my ambition to become a doctor. From then on I wanted to know how to save lives, how to make people well.'

She reached for her coffee and then sent him a

quick look. 'What about your family? Are they all well and living locally?'

'Yes, they're strong and full of life. My parents live about ten miles away, so I see them regularly, and I have a brother who works as an administrator for the hospitals in the area. He's married with a couple of children, and I visit with them quite often.'

Jordan broke off and searched her face, his mouth taking on a serious line. 'We ought to decide what we're going to do about you tonight. I think you should have someone stay with you until the alarm system is in place at least. Once the security is sorted out you'll probably feel safer, because at least it might give you time to phone for help if you need it—even if it just means phoning a neighbour. In the meantime, you shouldn't be on your own.'

'I'll get by.' She wasn't entirely convinced of that, but she wasn't going to admit to being afraid.

He shook his head. 'I could stay with you for to-night.' He saw her eyes widen and he must have heard the faint intake of her breath because he put up a hand to stop her protest. 'I'm sure you'll rest a bit more easily, knowing that someone else is around. It's no problem—presumably, I can sleep on the sofa.'

'There's no need for you to stay here,' she muttered. 'Besides, I don't want to drag you into all this.' In fact, she wasn't quite sure how she would handle having him around in such an intimate situation. She was beginning to realise that she was very much aware of him, both as a man and as her boss, and she wasn't sure she was ready for such close contact.

In fact, she wasn't ready to let down her guard with any man. She had made that mistake with Richard and it had let to all kinds of problems. She was still suffering from the after-effects.

'You don't have to feel that it's your responsibility to look after me,' she said quietly. 'There's no need for you to do anything. I'll be all right, really.'

He fixed her with a stern gaze. 'You can be a really stubborn woman sometimes, Abby. Why are you giving me such a hard time over this?'

'I prefer to think of it as being determined,' she said with a rueful smile. 'I've tried to be independent over the years, though if I need help, of course, I'll ask for it…but thank you for offering, all the same. Anyway, I'm not entirely defenceless. There are people who I can rely on to help if need be.'

Though exactly what Corinne could do if she was to phone her in a time of trouble, she had no idea.

He stared at her, a glint of something unreadable in his blue-grey eyes. 'I had forgotten that. Of course—you probably have someone close to you who would want to help out.'

Abby frowned for a moment, not quite understanding his guarded expression, but then she wondered if he supposed that there was someone else in her life. Did he think she had a man friend she would call on? She wasn't going to tell him any different…it wouldn't hurt for him to believe that she wasn't helpless or without other options, would it?

'I'm sure I'll manage,' she said, aiming for a tone that would convince herself as well as him. 'That reminds me,' she murmured, 'I ought to ring Jessica and explain that I won't be joining her. Would you excuse me for a minute or two while I do that? Help yourself to more coffee.'

Jordan's eyes narrowed on her, but he made no

comment. Aware of his cool gaze, she went over to the extension phone in the far corner of the room and perched on a bar stool while she made the call.

Jessica's friend, Jane, answered. 'Abby? I'm so glad you rang me. I was just about to call you for advice.'

'Oh? Why is that?' Abby was troubled by the note of unease in Jane's voice.

'It's just that I don't know what to do. You're a doctor, aren't you—as well as her friend? Jessica's ill, and I'm not sure what I ought to do for the best. I wanted to call for an ambulance, but she won't let me—she won't even let me call her GP because she says it's out of hours and he'll tell her it's a virus or something unimportant. She keeps saying she has to be here for Chloe.'

'What's wrong with her?'

'She's been very sick. I'm not sure, but I think she's been vomiting blood. She tried to keep me out of the bathroom, but I managed to get in there and something is really wrong, I know it. She's in a lot of pain and she's very pale. She fainted a few minutes ago.'

'I'll come over and take a look at her. Keep her warm and try to get her to sit still, or lie still, in whatever position she's most comfortable.' Abby paused. 'Is Chloe all right? Has she seen what's going on?'

'She's asleep. I put her to bed an hour ago.'

'Good. That's one less worry, at least. Tell me where you live, Jane, and I'll be with you as soon as I can.'

Abby put the phone down a moment later and looked around.

'Is there a problem?' Jordan asked.

She told him what Jane had said, and added, 'I need to find my road map. I'm not sure exactly how to find where she lives. It's the next village, east of here. Carter's Lane.'

'I know the area. I'll drive us there.'

Abby hesitated. A feeling of relief had washed over her at the offer, but she was wary all the same. Her instinct was to stay independent as far as possible, but she hadn't realised quite how much she needed a shoulder to lean on, someone to help her out. Tension had been building up in her all day, and now she had yet another difficult situation to contend with. She was worried about her friend, and she wanted to do her best for her. It sounded like an emergency situation and, whereas at the hospital she could always rely on back-up, out here she had no one to depend on but herself.

She said softly, 'I don't want to put you to any trouble…I'm sure I'll find it.' She was afraid of involving Jordan too much in her personal life. He was her boss, and she wasn't altogether sure it would be a good thing.

'I said I would drive you there,' he said tersely. 'I wish you would just accept my help, instead of giving me so many arguments. If she's in a bad way, she might need two of us to help her. Shall we get going, or are you going to waste more time arguing with me?'

He could be right, she supposed. What if she needed help with Jessica?

She conceded the point with good grace, and he drove her there as fast as was possible, his car smoothly covering the miles to Jane's house. As soon

as they arrived, Jane took them up to the main bedroom where Jessica was lying down, and Abby introduced herself and Jordan.

Jessica looked as though she was in a bad way. 'I
need to examine you, Jessica,' Abby said. 'Are you
in a lot of pain?'

Jessica nodded. 'It hurts if I move.'

Abby quickly examined her, being as gentle as she
could. 'Have you been sick?' she asked, and again
Jessica nodded. 'Was there any blood in it? It's really
important that I know exactly what's been happening.'

'Yes. It's been going on for a while now,' Jessica
managed. 'The sickness and the stomach pain. I don't
know what's the matter with me. It's something bad,
isn't it? But I can't be ill—I have to look after Chloe.
She needs me.'

'You won't be any good to Chloe like this,' Abby
said firmly. 'You must let us treat you. You should
be in hospital.'

'I don't want to go to hospital.' Jessica was white-
faced, her lips taut with pain.

'I know you don't, but we can't treat you properly
here. I suspect you have a perforated stomach ulcer
and that it's haemorrhaging, but we won't know for
sure until we do some tests. You must let us take care
of you now.'

'But what's going to happen to Chloe? She can't
go to her father. He won't look after her properly, and
I won't let her go into care.'

'We'll work something out,' Abby said. 'I'm sure
Jane won't mind keeping her here for tonight, and
we'll think about what other options we have in the

morning. If you want to be around to look after Chloe, you must let us take you to hospital now.'

Jessica closed her eyes briefly, then whispered, 'All right...but promise me you won't let them put her into care.'

Jordan called for an ambulance, and Abby said quietly, 'I promise I'll work something out. Now, let's get on with making you more comfortable.' She looked up at Jordan. 'I'm going to put an IV line in. I'll give her saline to replace the volume she's lost and morphine for the pain.'

He came over to her, and as she worked he said in a low voice, 'She'll need cyclizine to stop her from being sick, and antibiotics as well. If there's a perforation, it could be bad news.'

'I know,' Abby said worriedly. 'And from the look of her, the bleeding is not going to stop on its own.'

'I'll make arrangements for her to have an endoscopy as soon as we get her to the hospital. That should tell us what's going on.'

The paramedics arrived within minutes and by then the morphine was helping to subdue some of Jessica's pain. They transferred her by stretcher to the ambulance, and Abby and Jordan followed in his car.

'What made you think she has a perforated ulcer?' Jordan asked, sending Abby an oblique glance. 'Has she had symptoms of ulceration before this?'

'Well, I haven't known her very long but I think she has. She had been sick a lot and has complained of pain in her stomach. I think she tried over-the-counter remedies, as well as something the doctor gave her, but they weren't much use to her. She keeps things to herself a lot of the time, and tries to pretend everything is all right for Chloe's sake, but she has obviously been under a lot of stress. She has problems with her ex-husband and she's trying to bring Chloe up alone. Daniel's away, and then the business last night can't have helped.'

'It wasn't good for either of you.'

'No. Well, as soon as I get the chance, I'll get some security systems put in for both of us, and do what I can to help her when she comes out of hospital.'

'That's not likely to be any time soon, from the looks of her.' Jordan swung the car into the hospital car park. 'Let's go and see how she is. I know that you're worried about her.'

Within a short time of Jessica arriving at the hospital, the emergency team was doing tests to find out what was wrong with her. Blood tests would give clues to what was going on, and they also cross-matched blood in case she needed a transfusion.

Abby and Jordan waited while Mike, the doctor in charge, used an endoscope to look into Jessica's stomach and duodenum to find out whether there was any ulceration and to pinpoint where the bleeding was coming from.

'There's an area of ulceration here,' Mike pointed out, indicating the monitor as he worked, 'and it's bleeding at the base. I'll use the endoscope to try to stop that. It's one of the most effective methods we have, and it's probably preferable to surgery.'

He worked quickly to stem the bleeding, and after a while he murmured with satisfaction, 'That seems to have stopped it. We'll give her antibiotics, as Jordan suggested—cefuroxime and metronidazole— and she'll need a blood transfusion.'

When Jessica was feeling in slightly better shape, Jordan told her, 'We're going to arrange for you to be admitted to hospital so that we can deal with the cause of the ulceration and the anaemia.'

'Anaemia?' Jessica echoed huskily.

'You've lost a lot of blood, and it's probably been going on for some time before this. It's important that you get your strength back. You're very poorly, young lady, and you need to be looked after for a while.'

A porter came to take Jessica up to a ward, and Mike came over to Jordan and Abby and spoke quietly to them. 'I think it would be a good idea to contact her family, so that they can support her through this. She's been under a lot of strain, from the looks of things, and she can't go on that way. Do you have an address for her parents?'

Abby shook her head. 'I don't, I'm afraid. They fell out with her some time ago and haven't had much to do with her since her marriage. I don't know their surname, but her maiden name might be on file. She said they live a few miles away.'

Abby wondered how Jessica's parents could have stayed away for so long. Did they even know that they had a grandchild? Surely they would want to see her? But perhaps the barrier that had gone up between them and their daughter had been too hard to break down. Jessica had probably wanted to prove to herself that she could cope perfectly well without them and was loath to make the first move.

'I'll see what the welfare advisor can find out,' Mike murmured. 'Your friend's going to be under par for a while yet, and she'll need someone standing by when she gets home. With endoscopy haemostasis there's less chance of another bleed, but if she develops more ulceration, who knows?'

Abby nodded. Poor Jessica. She made up her mind to contact her brother at the first opportunity and let him know what was happening.

Abby went to the ward to see Jessica settle in, and Jordan waited for her just a short distance away as she said goodbye to her friend.

'I'll come and see you tomorrow,' Abby promised. 'I'm sure you'll be feeling much better by then.'

Drained, Jessica found the strength to reach for her hand. 'Promise me you'll look after Chloe for me. You won't let anyone take her away from me?'

'I promise,' Abby murmured. 'I'll see to it that she goes to nursery school tomorrow, and I'll ask Corinne to watch her until I get home from work. She can stay at my house until you're well again. Don't worry about anything, Jessica. I'll take care of things for you.'

'Thank you.' For the first time since her ordeal began, Jessica seemed to relax a little. Her eyes closed, and she allowed her exhausted body to drift into sleep.

Jordan and Abby walked back to his car. 'You can't seriously be thinking of looking after a four-year-old child,' he said with a frown as he helped her into the passenger seat.

'I'm very serious about it,' she told him. 'You could see for yourself what a state she was in. She would never have let herself rest if she thought Chloe would be taken into care.'

'That's not your problem, though, is it?'

She threw him a determined glance. 'I'm making it mine. Besides, I promised my brother that I would look after Jessica and Chloe, and he wouldn't thank me for letting them suffer in any way. I mean to do exactly as I said.'

'You haven't given yourself time to think it through properly,' Jordan persisted, starting the engine and driving away from the hospital. 'You have a job of work to do, and it's difficult enough to cope with that, without burdening yourself with caring for a young child as well.'

'I won't let it interfere with my work,' she said tautly. 'You won't have any cause to complain.'

His mouth made a grim line. 'That remains to be seen, doesn't it?'

When they arrived back at her house, he said crisply, 'Come on, let's go and see you inside. Perhaps you should let me check that everything's OK in there.'

'Thanks, I'd appreciate that,' she murmured, and stood back to let him through the front door. If the truth were told, she was beginning to feel a little nervous about returning to a dark, empty house, but she wasn't going to let him know that.

He made a thorough search, and pronounced that all was well. 'My offer still holds,' he said. 'You have only to say the word, and I'll stay here with you tonight to make sure that you're all right.'

She was tempted to take him up on that, but he was already annoyed with her over Chloe and she didn't want to give him the chance to try to change her mind. In the end, he would only be let down by her refusal, and she didn't want to make things awkward between them at work. Her position was difficult enough as it was.

She shook her head. 'I've taken up enough of your time this evening. Thanks for all you've done to help me with Jessica. It was really good of you, and I'm very grateful, but I'll be fine now, really.'

He accepted her decision with narrowed eyes, and she guessed he assumed that she would be calling on a boyfriend to help out. The thought made her grimace faintly. If it was at all possible for her to stand on her own two feet and deal with situations, that was what she would do. The days were gone when she would let a man take over her life.

Thankfully, the rest of the night passed without incident, and in the morning she picked up Chloe from Jane's house and dropped her off at nursery school. To Abby's relief, the little girl seemed to accept her explanation that her mother wasn't feeling very well and was resting in hospital, and she went off happily enough to join her friends.

Jordan was with a patient in A and E when Abby's shift began, and she was kept busy throughout the morning, so that there was little time for chatting.

When she managed to get five minutes for a coffee-break later on, she decided to send an e-mail to Daniel, telling him about Jessica.

Once she had done that, she quickly scanned her own messages. Most were work-orientated, but there was one that stood out from all the others. It was a personal message, and it read simply, 'I miss you, Abby, and I can't wait to see you again... Call me. You know how much I love you. Richard.'

Abby stared at the screen in front of her. How had he managed to find her so soon? She had asked colleagues at her last hospital not to reveal her e-mail or physical address to anyone, and she trusted them implicitly.

She had tried so hard to put some distance between

herself and Richard, and now it looked as though all her efforts had been in vain.

How had he done it? How could he have found out where she was?

There was only one way that she could think of. Perhaps he had guessed she would want to be close to her family. He didn't know her brother's address, but he knew the area where he lived and he could have tracked him down eventually. Richard would realise that Abby needed to find work. From there it wouldn't have taken much checking to find out which hospital she was working at.

'Is everything all right?' She looked up to find Jordan standing beside her. He towered over her, immaculate in a beautifully tailored grey suit, his jacket open, and beneath it his blue shirt was crisp and fresh-looking.

She blinked and tried to gather her wits. 'Oh… Yes…everything's fine, thanks.'

He looked at her quizzically, his blue-grey eyes scanning her features. 'You had no problems last night, then?'

She shook her head. 'None at all…'

In fact, she had been so tired that she had fallen into a deep sleep as soon as she had got to bed.

It was only just now that her worries had started up again, taking off in another direction altogether. But it could be that, where Richard was concerned, she was simply assuming too much. There wasn't necessarily a problem here. Her nerves had been stretched almost to the limit lately and, when all things were considered, it was just an e-mail after all, and a harmless one at that.

Richard had a job, an important job as a researcher,

and he couldn't just up and leave on a whim. He wouldn't come after her. He was probably still in London, and she was getting herself worked up over nothing. As soon as she had a chance, she would e-mail him back and tell him to stop trying to get in touch with her.

'Have you done anything about getting your security systems upgraded?'

Jordan was leaning negligently against the desk, one long leg stretched out, the other slightly bent, and she couldn't help but see the way the fabric of his trousers stretched against the hard muscle of his thigh. She frowned. She felt hot all over.

He gave her a hard stare. 'If not, I can start the ball rolling for you. I know a good company that will do the work quickly and well.'

His nearness was playing havoc with her nervous system. Abby pulled herself together and said quickly, 'No...there's no need for you to do that. I phoned around this morning to arrange for a security firm to come and fit an alarm and lights, and they said they would sort it out for me as soon as possible—this evening, probably.'

He nodded, satisfied. 'That's good. And Jessica?'

'I rang the ward and spoke to the sister in charge a couple of hours ago. She's sore and uncomfortable, but they're making sure that she rests and they're keeping an eye on her to make sure there's no recurrence of the bleeding. She was very anaemic, and her condition needs monitoring.'

She grimaced. 'She won't rest easy while she's separated from Chloe, but her condition is stable, at least.'

'I'm glad to hear it. You must let me know if she

needs anything. I'll do whatever I can to help, medically or otherwise. It must be difficult for her, being on her own.'

'I'm sure she'll appreciate that.' Abby stretched, easing her tense muscles, and ran a hand through the tumbled array of bright curls that strayed across her cheek, pushing them away from her face.

Jordan's glance followed the movement of her hand, then roamed over her, tracing the soft curve of her breast, outlined by the clinging top she wore, and drifting down over her snug-fitting skirt to where the long shapeliness of her legs was revealed.

'Are you feeling better about things?' he asked. 'You certainly looked more relaxed when you arrived at the hospital this morning.'

'Did I?' She looked away, confused by his sudden searing scrutiny. 'I haven't really had time to dwell on what happened, with one thing and another.'

'No,' he said after a moment or two, and she realised that his tone had changed. He straightened up. 'I expect you've been preoccupied.' His voice was tinged with irony, and she glanced up at him and saw that his gaze was resting on the computer screen and the message from Richard.

No doubt he believed she had found someone who was willing to soothe her fears. She grimaced. If only he knew...

CHAPTER FIVE

CHLOE stayed at Abby's house for the next few days. Abby went and fetched her clothes from next door, along with a selection of toys so that she would feel more at home. All in all, she felt that things were working out reasonably well, but it was clear that Chloe was missing her mother.

One night, Abby put her to bed in the small guest bedroom as usual. She sat with her and read her a bedtime story and then tucked her up with her teddy and her favourite doll, but the little girl was finding it difficult to settle.

'Stay wiv me,' Chloe said. 'Me not want sleep on my own.'

'I'm right here,' Abby told her gently, leaning over to stroke her soft curls. 'I'm not going anywhere. I'll stay here while you go to sleep.'

Chloe gradually closed her eyes, but every now and then she would open them to make sure that Abby was keeping her promise. 'When my mummy come home?' she asked.

'As soon as she's strong enough,' Abby said softly. She would have liked to have said that it would be soon, but Jessica was frail and in a bad way, and it would take some time for her to recover from the shock to her system.

'She still poorly?'

'She is, but she's getting better. I'll ask Mrs Matthews if she can bring you to see her at the hospital tomorrow if you like.' Corinne had already offered, and Abby thought it should be simple enough to arrange her off-duty time so that she could go with them to visit Jessica.

It took a while for Chloe to settle, but even then she woke a couple of times in the night, crying and waking Abby from a deep sleep.

Yawning, she got up and went into the little girl's room and soothed the child, feeling her forehead to see if she was ill, but her temperature seemed to be normal. Chloe was bound to be troubled with her mother still in hospital. It was only to be expected that she would suffer from a few nights of disturbed sleep.

When morning came, and it was time for Abby to go to work, she was feeling exhausted. How on earth was she going to get through the day and still be firing on all cylinders?

She gulped down a quick cup of coffee with her breakfast, and hoped that it would wake her up a little. A few minutes later, she dropped Chloe off at Corinne's house. Corinne would take her to nursery school and bring her to the hospital later in the afternoon, and the little girl was bubbly with excitement at the prospect.

Jordan slanted a glance over Abby as soon as she walked into A and E. 'You look as though you've been burning the candle at both ends,' he remarked grimly. 'There are dark shadows under your eyes. Are they from lack of sleep—or are you ill?'

She made a wry face. Did the man never miss anything? 'Do I really look that bad?' she muttered. She had hoped a light touch of make-up would hide any blemishes, but obviously she hadn't succeeded. 'I'm perfectly well, thanks. You've no need to worry—I'm sure I shan't give you any cause for concern.'

'I hope that's true.' His gaze narrowed on her. 'This is an exacting job, and it isn't compatible with a demanding social life. You can't give your best if you've been up half the night clubbing, or whatever.'

'You should know I've hardly any time for club-bing...or for "whatever",' Abby retorted, 'not with all the studying I have to do to keep on top of all the new and unusual conditions I come across in A and E. Anyway, I have a four-year-old chaperone now, remember. She's very good at helping to curb my wild side.'

Her sarcasm didn't have the effect that she had ex-pected. Instead of laughing off his misinterpretation of her night-time activities, Jordan studied her even more keenly than before. 'It's been more than a week, hasn't it? Has she been staying with you the whole time? What about her grandparents?'

'Social Services hasn't managed to find them yet, and even if they do, it isn't going to be a solution if they haven't had any contact with their daughter or their granddaughter for years. So, yes, she's been with me since Jessica came into hospital.'

'How is she coping?'

Abby stretched sinuously, easing her tense muscles. 'She was all right at first, but now I think she's be-ginning to really miss her mother. She's been used to seeing her at the end of the day, and she's disap-pointed when she doesn't come and fetch her from school. She often asks about her.'

'It must be hard for her to understand,' he agreed, with a grimace. 'They've been together for all her young life, just Chloe and Jessica, with no father or grandparents around, and now everything has suddenly changed. The child must be very confused.'

'She's managed well enough up to now. I'm going to take her to see her mother this afternoon, but to be honest I don't know whether that will help or just serve to make matters worse. She might be even more upset at being parted from her again.'

'It can't be good for either of them to be kept apart for any length of time, though. The usual policy is to try to keep parents and children together as much as possible, though it isn't so easy when it's the parent who's ill.' He scanned her features. 'It doesn't look as though it's doing you much good either. Did she have a bad night?'

Abby nodded. 'I hope she's not coming down with something, but so far she seems to be healthy enough.'

'You can't tell with little ones. One minute they're up, the next they're down. Can't you reconsider your options and find someone else to take care of her?'

Abby shook her head. 'I'm not prepared to do that,' she said firmly. 'She's a dear little soul and I like having her around. Anyway, I promised Jessica, and I gave my word to my brother that I would watch out for both of them. I'm not going to let any of them down just because things start to get a little difficult.'

'You certainly have staying power, I'll give you that,' Jordan said drily. 'Given the circumstances, let's hope it filters through to your work as well.' He moved away to tend to a patient, leaving her to get to grips with the day's work.

She stared after him. When it came down to it, he was always her boss, first and foremost, wasn't he? Abby reflected grimly. She would never be able to forget that. Trying to quell the surge of irritation he had provoked in her, she picked up a patient's chart and went to deal with someone's lacerated hand.

In the afternoon, she and Corinne took Chloe to visit her mother. Jessica was still weak and she was being given antibiotics to combat an infection that had taken hold of her despite their attempts to avert the danger, but it was clear that she was overjoyed to see her small daughter.

She and Chloe hugged each other, and Chloe sat on her bed and showed her mother all the things that she had been making for her over the last few days at home and at school. She had been learning her phonetics at nursery school and now she presented Jessica with a page of squiggles and a picture of her mother, a round, smiling face with long pencilled legs and arms.

'It says, "I love you mummy",' Chloe said, pointing to the various crayon marks. 'You come home soon?'

'Soon,' Jessica agreed. She looked pale and tired, and she leaned back against her pillows, her arm around Chloe, while she looked at her drawings.

Chloe protested when she had to leave her at the end of visiting time, and Abby didn't know who she wanted to comfort most, Jessica or her child. Jessica's eyes were bright with tears as they said goodbye, and Chloe's bottom lip was trembling.

Chloe had another bad night, and for the second day in a row Abby turned up at work looking the worse for wear. Luckily, Jordan wasn't there to see her this time.

'He's at a meeting this morning with management,'

Sarah told her. 'Something to do with the hospital budget.'

Abby pulled a face. 'Don't tell me they're after finding more ways of trying to make us work even harder?'

Still, at least she could relax a little while he wasn't around. Whenever Jordan was close by, she found that she was conscious of him the whole time. It wasn't just that he was in charge, it was his sheer male presence, the fact that she couldn't help but be aware of his lithe movements, of his strong, angular features and the way he smiled or grimaced...the fact that he was simply there.

She forced herself to push him from her mind and attend to the business in hand.

'There's a patient coming in,' Sarah announced an hour or so later. 'Her husband called for an ambulance. She has severe chills, high fever and shortness of breath. We're expecting her to be here in about five minutes.'

Abby was struggling to fend off tiredness. She finished off a cup of coffee and eased back her shoulders in an attempt to loosen her aching sinews, then prepared herself to receive the patient.

She was a woman in her forties, her brown hair lying damply against her hot brow. She was in pain and finding it difficult to breathe.

'I'm going to listen to your chest, Laura,' Abby said, taking out her stethoscope and listening to the woman's breath sounds.

'There's an irregular heartbeat,' she said quietly to Sarah a few minutes later as they stood to one side of the trolley where the woman lay, propped up by pillows. 'We'd better do blood tests, as well as an echocardiograph. We'll get a chest X-ray as well. There could be an infection of some sort, but until we get the results back, we're in the dark. Tell the lab we need the answers as soon as possible.'

She gently questioned her patient about previous infections and illnesses, but the woman was tiring rapidly and finding it hard to concentrate.

'You should lie back and rest,' Abby told her.

She went to speak to the husband who was pacing anxiously in the waiting room. 'I'm going to monitor your wife's condition over the next hour or so, Mr Tennant. She's very poorly, and she has a heart murmur that I'm concerned about, but I'll have a better idea of what's causing her problems when I have the results of the blood tests. Has she had any infections recently, anything at all that you can think of?'

He shook his head. 'She's never been very strong. She has a lung complaint that tends to pull her down.'

Abby had seen that in the notes, but she didn't believe at this stage that Laura's lung complaint would be causing the symptoms she had now. 'Is there anything else you can think of?' she persisted.

He frowned. 'The only thing she complained about was an abscess that came up on her leg. She thought she must have caught herself on something or been bitten by something. It was troublesome, and I told her she ought to see a doctor about it, but we're on holiday, and she didn't want the hassle. She wanted to be out and about, not waiting around in a health centre.' He paused, staring at Abby. 'Surely an abscess can't have anything to do with what's happening now?'

'We don't know at this stage, but I have to investigate everything,' Abby told him. 'Thank you for your help.'

Abby nodded towards a fair-haired young nurse, waiting a short distance away. 'If you go along with Nicole, she'll show you where you can wait. She'll go through some forms with you while we attend to your wife.'

Abby went back to her patient and carefully examined her once more. She discovered the inflamed and infected abscess on Laura's right calf, and quickly took a swab for analysis by the laboratory. She was annoyed with herself for not having noticed it before. Was tiredness affecting her ability to think clearly?

'I think you have an infection which is making you ill,' Abby told Laura. 'We need to do tests to find out the exact cause of your illness, but in the meantime I'm going to start you off on antibiotics to try to deal with the infection.'

She turned to Sarah and said in a low voice, 'I'm going to put an IV line in and treat her with benzyl-penicillin and gentamicin.'

A few minutes later, after making sure that the woman was comfortable, she left her with Sarah, who took blood samples and carried out an ECG. While that was being done, Abby went to check up on her other patients.

The day progressed, and she was dealing with a young man's fractured finger when Nicole came into the cubicle and said, 'Your neighbour's here with Chloe. The little girl's running a temperature and is asking for you. She seems quite distressed.'

Abby's heart began to thump. Chloe was feverish? The child hadn't had a good night, but she had seemed all right this morning, apart from asking for her mother. Surely she couldn't have missed something? What kind of doctor was she if she couldn't even see that a child she was caring for in her own home was ill?

'Thanks, Nicole,' she said quietly, trying to keep her agitation under control. 'Would you take over for me here, please? Mr Draycott has a fractured finger, and I've almost finished strapping it up for him.'

'Of course.' Nicole came and sat down beside the man and continued with the bandaging.

Abby hurried to find Chloe. She was at the far end of the room, and her little face was crumpled, tears slowly coursing down her cheeks. When she saw Abby, she came towards her, arms reaching out to her.

Corinne said, 'I hope you don't mind me bringing her here. The school called me to come and fetch her, and I would have taken her to the doctor, but the surgery is closed for a half-day from lunchtime, and she was desperate to see you.'

'That's all right, Corinne. Don't worry. You did the right thing.'

Abby knelt down and gave Chloe a big hug. 'What's wrong, sweetheart? Aren't you feeling very well?'

Chloe shook her head and put a hand to her ear. 'Hurts,' she said miserably. 'Abby make it better?'

'I'll see what I can do, shall I? Let me have a look.'

Corinne sat down with the little girl on her lap while Abby looked in the ear with an auriscope. Then she checked the other ear, and said, 'It's no wonder you're hurting, Chloe. You've an infection in your ear and that's why it hurts so much. I'll give you some medicine to make it better.'

She gave the girl a cuddle and said to Corinne, 'You can give her Calpol as well, to ease the pain. Poor little thing, no wonder she was so upset.'

She looked up to see Jordan walk into A and E, and just then Sarah came to her and said quickly, 'Your patient has taken a turn for the worse. Laura Tennant—she's going downhill fast.'

'I'll come and see her.' Abby glanced at Corinne. She didn't want to leave Chloe like this, but she had no choice. 'Will you be all right with Chloe?'

'Yes, of course. You go and get on, love.' She looked down at Chloe. 'Come on, chick. We'll go home now.'

'Me no want go home,' Chloe wailed, and dug her heels into the ground. Abby ran a hand distractedly through her hair. More than anything, she wanted to hold the child and soothe her tears away.

Jordan was giving her a hard stare, and she wondered if he was annoyed because she was spending time with the little girl when her patients needed her.

'I know you don't, Chloe,' she said softly. 'I wonder... Perhaps...' She sent Corinne a quick look. 'Would you have time to go up to Rose Ward?'

'To see her mum, you mean?' Corinne nodded. 'That's a good idea. I'll go and get this prescription filled first, and then we'll go and pay her a visit.'

'Would you like to go and see your mummy?' Abby asked.

Chloe's tears began to subside. She nodded. 'We go now?'

'Yes, chick,' Corinne said. 'As soon as we've fetched your medicine.'

Abby gave the child another hug and said goodbye, then hurried off to look at Laura. Examining her, she found that her heart murmur had changed and she was showing signs of heart failure.

'Let's get her on oxygen,' she told Sarah. Anxiously, she debated her next course of action.

'What's the situation here?' Jordan asked, startling her out of her worried deliberations. He had appeared out of nowhere, and now he was busily scanning her patient's chart.

She moved away from the trolley so that Laura couldn't hear their discussion. 'She presented with signs of infection that was affecting her heart,' she said in an undertone. 'I've put her on antibiotic therapy, but I'm still waiting for results from the lab.'

'In the meantime, she's getting progressively worse and showing signs of heart failure.' He frowned, his mouth making a straight line, and Abby's self-confidence plummeted.

'Should I have tried something different?'

'You could put her on flucloxacillin. If it's a staphylococcal infection it should help. Some bacteria are resistant to a variety of antibiotics, but so far there's a good chance that flucloxacillin should do the trick. That's if it isn't too late. She may already have a valve failure.'

His expression was grim, and Abby drew in an anxious breath. Had she let her patient down?

'I'll see to it straight away.' She gave Sarah instructions to start the antibiotic and asked her to monitor the patient closely.

'What was Chloe doing here?' Jordan asked. 'Shouldn't she be at school?'

'She has an ear infection,' Abby said unhappily. 'That must be what was keeping her awake the last couple of nights.'

'She's not had much luck lately, has she?'

Abby shook her head, and Nicole came to find her at that moment. 'Your man with the head injury is complaining of double vision.'

Abby sucked in another breath and followed Nicole to the cubicle. Could this day possibly get any worse?

A short time later it seemed that it could. 'Mrs Tennant's heart failure is progressing,' Sarah said urgently.

Abby went to examine the woman once more. 'Is there still no result from the lab?' she asked the nurse, as she ran her stethoscope over Laura's chest and listened to her heart.

Sarah shook her head.

'It looks as though the infection has damaged the heart valve,' Abby said. 'We'd better call for Mr Johnson to do an emergency valve replacement.'

'She'll need extra antibiotic cover for that,' Jordan said, appearing at her side. 'Put her on vancomycin.'

Abby nodded. Just a few minutes later, Laura was being wheeled up to Theatre and Abby fled to the doctors' lounge to fight back the tears that were beginning to well up in her eyes. It was unbearable to think that she might have been in any way responsible for allowing the poor woman's health to deteriorate in such a devastating way.

'Abby?' She had her back turned to the door, but Jordan's deep voice sounded a cautious note in her ears. She heard him cross the room and come towards her, and quickly she dashed the dampness from her eyes with the back of her hand. 'Is everything OK?' he asked.

'Yes... I was just grabbing a coffee while things are quiet,' she mumbled into the wall in front of her.

She would have reached for the coffee-pot but her hand was shaking so much that she was afraid that he would see and despise her for her weakness.

He laid his hands on her shoulders, cupping them, and slowly he turned her around.

'You're upset. What's wrong?'

She swallowed hard. 'It's been a difficult day, that's all... My patient's undergoing surgery, and I ought to have been able to forestall that. Then Chloe turned up here, feverish and unhappy, and I feel responsible for that, too. I should have seen that something was wrong with her.'

'Why should you? I saw her yesterday and there didn't seem to be much wrong with her then. What makes you think you should be omnipotent all of a sudden? You're human. You can't be aware of every subtle change in the people around you every minute of the day and, besides, Chloe was upset about her mother being in hospital. She's only four, and it would be easy enough to mistake her fretfulness for worries about her mother.'

'I'm a doctor. I should have known something was wrong, just as I should have known what to do for Laura Tennant. I didn't act quickly enough. I let things slide, and now she's paying the consequences.' Her mouth trembled, and she pressed her lips together to stop it from happening.

'It isn't your fault,' Jordan said firmly. 'You did what you could in the time available. You followed all the correct procedures, but the infection is a virulent one and it progressed too rapidly for any of the measures to take effect. You couldn't have done anything differently.'

'I should have chosen another type of antibiotic. I

should have known that there were other things I could try. You knew what to do…'

He shook his head. 'Without the test results, we're both working in the dark. With Mrs Tennant's condition, there's a thirty per cent chance of mortality and there's no reason to suppose that my choice of antibiotic is any better than yours. You shouldn't whip yourself like this. Neither of us can do any more until we get those results back from the lab, and they're working on it as fast as they can.'

'Even so, I can't help feeling that I'm to blame.' Her eyes flooded with tears again, and he reached up and gently brushed them away with his thumb. Then, out of the blue, he tilted her chin with his cupped hand and dropped a tender kiss on her parted lips.

She stared at him in startled wonder. He had kissed her. Jordan had kissed her and it seemed as though the world had suddenly stopped its spinning and she was floating in suspended animation.

'You're tired,' he said softly, gazing into her shimmering eyes. 'You're taking the weight of the world on your shoulders, and it's an impossible task. Stop trying so hard. You have to learn to live with the way things are or you'll be burned out before too many more years have passed.'

Abby's eyes widened, her tremulous lips still registering the imprint of his mouth on hers, and her heart began to thud heavily as she realised that she had been lost for a moment, lost in a place where absolutely nothing mattered except that Jordan was holding her.

Watching her, he smiled faintly, then bent his head and kissed her again, slowly this time, savouring the softness of her mouth, brushing her lips lightly with his own. It was the gentlest touch, but it sent fiery sensation through the entire length of her body from head to toe.

She was lost for words, her limbs weak, languid with sudden, unexpected desire, and when he stepped back from her she felt dazed. She almost swayed towards him. She didn't know why he had stopped, when all she wanted was for the kiss to go on and on. Then she heard a sound from across the room and her mind juddered back to reality as though someone had flicked a switch.

The door to the lounge opened and Sarah came into the room. By then, Jordan had turned around and was already walking towards the door, and Abby wondered whether he had heard Sarah's approach or seen the shadow of her figure against the glass of the door.

In any case, he had gathered his wits in time to save them both from discovery.

Or perhaps he had not lost any sense of time and place as Abby had. He had been comforting her, trying to spur her out of her melancholy, and maybe the incident had meant absolutely nothing to him. Certainly he was behaving as though nothing had happened.

Sarah said, 'Jordan, there's a patient coming in by ambulance.'

'What's the problem?'

Abby made a determined effort to pull herself together and looked along the worktop to where the coffee-pot was gently steaming. She reached for the jug and was surprised to see that this time her hand was steady. Jordan had shocked her out of her fear and dismay, and perhaps that was what he had intended to do all along.

'It looks like a coronary thrombosis,' Sarah answered. 'They should be here in about eight minutes.'

'Thanks, Sarah.'

Sarah looked across at Abby. 'I thought you would like to know—Mrs Tennant's results are back from the lab. I've rung them through to Theatre.'

'Good. That's a relief,' Abby said. 'Let's hope Mrs Tennant comes through this all right.'

Sarah left the room a moment later, and Abby felt fairly confident that she hadn't noticed anything amiss.

She looked at Jordan, and he said briskly, 'I have to go and see to my patient. Stop worrying about things you can't put right. You do what you can, and that's all anyone can ask of any of us.'

He was cool and self-contained and totally professional once more. There was absolutely no hint in his manner that anything had happened between them.

Then he turned and left the room without looking back, leaving her to stare blankly after him. She didn't understand him at all. How could he have undergone such a mood change in just a few short minutes? Her world had been turned upside down, but as far as he was concerned it was just as though he had never kissed her.

CHAPTER SIX

ABBY had just arrived at the hospital car park a few days later and was locking up her car when Jordan came over to her. He flicked his key in the direction of his own sleek vehicle and activated the alarm system.

'You look more like your usual self today,' he said, running a fleeting glance over her, and she returned his gaze, her brow furrowing.

'Do I?' She brushed a hand over her hip, along the line of her slim-fitting skirt, as though to smooth out any imaginary crease, until she looked up and realised that his blue-grey eyes were watching her every move.

She stilled her hand. He was long and lithe, as full of vigour as ever. He always looked good. Today he was wearing an impeccably tailored dark grey suit, the jacket sitting well on his broad shoulders, and as usual it was open so that she could see the blue shirt beneath. His trousers were a perfect fit, moulding his hips and emphasising his long legs.

He nodded. 'You seem less harassed, and the hunted look has gone.' He smiled at her, and she caught the full impact of his attractive features. Something strange happened to her insides. Since that day when he had kissed her, she had been more intensely aware of him than ever before, but he had made no mention of it. It was as though it had never happened.

Now, he murmured, 'You must have had a better night than some of those recently. Does that mean Chloe's on the mend?'

'She's much better, thanks,' Abby said, returning the smile as they walked through the main entrance of the hospital. 'She's beginning to get over her ear infection. The pain and fever seem to have subsided, so she's a lot happier, and we're both getting a better night's sleep.'

'Are you coping all right? Things can't be easy for you, looking after a small child as well as doing a full-time job.'

'It took some getting used to,' she admitted with a small laugh. 'I don't have any nephews and nieces, so the only experience I've had with children is through my married friends. I think I'm beginning to get the hang of it. I like Chloe. She's a lovely little girl, and we seem to get along well together.'

'I could see that you do,' he said lightly. 'She's very natural with you and, apart from her mother, you were the one she wanted to be with when she was feeling poorly. Has she been to see her mother again?'

Abby nodded. 'Yes. Between us, Corinne and I are trying to make sure that she sees her every day. It's doing them both good to have that contact.'

Sarah was already in A and E when they walked into the department, and Abby could tell that she was bubbling over with excitement about something. She rushed straight over to them.

'You should see what's arrived for you this morning,' she said to Abby in a cheerful tone. 'I couldn't believe my eyes when Nicole showed me.'

'Showed you what?' Abby had no idea what she

was talking about. 'I wasn't expecting anything—unless it's lab results.'

Sarah laughed. 'No, it's not lab results. Come and see.'

Abby followed her into the doctors' lounge and blinked in amazement at the huge bouquet of flowers that Nicole had placed in water in the sink.

'They're beautiful, aren't they?' Sarah said, her eyes shining.

Abby stared at them. She couldn't imagine who would have sent her such lovely flowers.

'They are.' There was a breathtaking cascade of yellow roses, pink carnations and pale mauve irises set out against a background of green foliage. Interspersed among the greenery there were sprigs of gypsophila, and at the front there were delicate freesias, whose subtle fragrance filled the air. Abby swallowed hard. 'Are you sure they're for me?'

'Definitely. Read the card and see. He must be really keen to send you these…' Sarah rolled her eyes. 'And all this time you've been keeping him to yourself,' she said teasingly. 'You are a dark one.'

Abby shook her head and looked at the card that nestled among the blooms. 'Don't you know how much you mean to me?' the message read. 'You're my whole world, and I want to see you again, soon, very soon. Please don't make me wait. Love, Richard.'

A shiver ran through Abby. Richard. Again. She had e-mailed him, telling him to stay out of her life, and this was the result. It had been a mistake, answering him. He wasn't going to let go, was he?

Would she ever be free of him? Even now, after all that she had said to him in the past, after she had put so much distance between them, he still wasn't getting the message. He was pursuing her, coming steadily after her like a juggernaut that couldn't be stopped.

'Sarah's right,' Jordan's voice sounded dispassionately in her ear. 'The man's definitely ultra-keen.' He was reading the card, written in bold, black writing. 'Shouldn't you put him out of his misery and stop stringing him along?'

She glanced up at him and caught the sardonic glint in his eyes as his gaze meshed with hers. Outside, in the car park, he had been warm and friendly and she had been drawn to him all over again, but now things had changed and his manner was distinctly cool towards her. It was as though a light had gone out and she was plunged into darkness.

'I'll think about it,' she said in a low voice.

He looked back at the flowers and Abby did the same, her spirits sinking to an all-time low.

They were completely over the top, she had recognised that as soon as she had seen them. There were masses of blooms, and they were all flawless, but they were a gesture, a warning, Richard's way of making sure that everyone would know that she belonged to him. They were his way of telling her that he was never going to give up, and she recalled with a shudder that he had said she would regret leaving him. Knowing his tendency towards violence, she was afraid.

'You're so calm and matter-of-fact about it,' Sarah said, shaking her head in disbelief. 'I think I would be over the moon if someone made a gesture like this for me.'

Sarah clearly expected her to be ecstatic, to be dancing about with joy.

'Abby keeps her feelings locked up inside her,' Jordan said drily. 'She doesn't tell the world what she's thinking. Perhaps that's half her trouble.'

Abby could see the irony of that. If only she could talk to someone about how all this was affecting her...but how could she confide her fears to her friends and colleagues? They wouldn't understand how someone who had once been close to her was now able to fill her heart with dread by simply doing something that looked like an extravagant show of affection. Worse, Jordan would probably conclude that she had invited Richard's attentions by leading him on.

'I'm sure she's thrilled to bits really,' Sarah said cheerfully, 'but she's too awestruck to make a comment.' She turned to Abby. 'They must have cost him a small fortune. You'd best keep them somewhere cool so that they stay looking good when it comes to time to take them home with you.'

'Yes, I'll find somewhere to put them.'

As far as Abby was concerned, taking them home was not an option. Instead, grimacing inwardly, she decided that at the first opportunity she would get rid of the flowers. She couldn't drop them into the nearest bin, because that would invite too much comment, but perhaps she could divide them up into vases and distribute them around the wards. That way, no one would be any the wiser, and she need not reminded that they had been meant for her.

'Time to get ready for action, people.' Nicole arrived with news of incoming patients from a road traffic accident and Jordan swung away immediately to prepare for them. The whole team went on alert, and Abby was thankful that it took the pressure off her for a while.

'Is there any information on Mrs Tennant?' she asked Sarah later on. 'She was still in Intensive Care when I left here last night.'

'I heard they were thinking of moving her to the cardiac care ward some time today. The new valve seems to be working OK, and it looks as though the infection's coming under control now.'

'That's good.' Ever since the results had come through from the lab, the medical team had been giving the woman the most effective antibiotic for her condition and it looked as though she was beginning to respond to it at last.

'Yes. It's early days, of course, but the outlook seems fairly positive. At least no more damage seems to have been done.'

'I'm glad. That was scary for a while,' Abby said with feeling.

Sarah nodded, and must have guessed that Abby was suffering from waves of uncertainty because she added sympathetically, 'Feeling anxious about what's going on is all part of the job, you know. We're working at the sharp end, here in Accident and Emergency, but you do get used to it after a while. I've been in A and E for about three years, and I suppose I'm a lot tougher now than when I first started. It doesn't get any easier when you lose a patient or things go badly wrong, but at least you learn not to take it so personally.'

'Perhaps I'll feel like that in time, too.'

'You will, I'm sure.'

At the end of the day, when her shift finished, Abby

prepared to go home. She didn't really want to go back to the house, but there was Chloe to consider, and she didn't really have any choice.

'Has it been a bad day?' Jordan asked. His deep voice broke into her thoughts, and she glanced in the direction it came from.

He was in his office, sitting behind his desk dealing with a mound of paperwork, the door wide open so that he was available if needed. She guessed that he must have seen her hesitating and was wondering what her problem was. That was the thing about Jordan…he never seemed to miss anything.

'You were frowning,' he said. 'Is something bothering you?'

'I suppose I'm just feeling the after-effects of a long day. We're constantly making decisions that can affect people's lives, aren't we? Sometimes it feels as though the adrenaline is pumping the whole time.'

'It's a demanding job,' he murmured, his glance shifting over her. 'It's hardly surprising if you find yourself wilting at the end of the day. You need to go home and recharge your batteries.'

'I think you're right.' It was true that she felt physically tired, but it was more than that. She was mentally on edge, too, worrying about this business with Richard. Was he the prowler who had rummaged through her house? Was he intending to come back again?

Aware that Jordan was still looking at her, she pushed her worries aside. 'Is that what you're planning to do? To go home and relax?'

He made a wry smile. 'Not for a while yet. I still have some work to do, finishing off here. And then I have to do some research on the internet for a paper

I'm presenting at a conference. I shall be here for a couple more hours at least.'

'Is there anything I can do to help?' He looked weary, and she felt a sudden surge of sympathy wash over her for him. He had the responsibility for the whole department weighing on him and, though he never wavered or appeared to have any problem with that, it must be a heavy burden at times.

She said quietly, 'I have to go and fetch Chloe, but I could do some work for you later, if it would help. I can use the computer at home to do research for you, if you like.'

Jordan leaned back in his chair, his gaze running over her. 'That's a really generous offer, Abby, but I can manage, thanks.' He looked at her quizzically. 'Aren't you planning on seeing Richard this evening?' he asked.

She braced herself against the faint shiver that suddenly chilled her bones. 'No, I'm not planning on doing that.'

The very opposite, she thought, pressing her lips together. If only she knew what Richard intended. He was checking up on her whereabouts, infiltrating her workspace, and it was beginning to feel as though he was close by...but how likely was that? After all, the flowers that had arrived for her this morning had been delivered by a national organisation, and Richard was probably still firmly ensconced in London.

'You're not?' Jordan lifted a dark brow, and she guessed that he was finding it hard to believe her.

She shook her head. If she could have unburdened herself to him it might make her feel better, but that would probably turn out to be a mistake in the end. What could he do about her worries after all? More than likely he had problems of his own, and she would simply be adding to his own difficulties.

And anyway, he was her boss. His major concern would always be the effect her anxieties could have on her performance in A and E.

'Actually, I shall probably take Chloe to see her mother for a while and then, when we get home again and I've put Chloe to bed, my time's my own.'

'Then use it to unwind. You've done enough for one day.'

That was another irony, wasn't it? While she was busy at work she could at least try to push her problems to the back of her mind, but they were never far away. They were always lurking, ready to surface at any moment.

Jordan had returned to his paperwork and, feeling that his mind was elsewhere, Abby reluctantly turned away and set off for home.

She gave Chloe her tea, and then took her to see her mother at the hospital. Abby was pleased to see that Jessica's condition was improving.

She cuddled her daughter and looked at a storybook with her, then said to Abby, 'They told me I had to stay in hospital for longer than usual because of the infection, but it looks as though that's beginning to clear up now. I'm hoping that means I'll be able to come home soon...after a few days, anyway. The doctor said it depends on whether my anaemia's under control, and whether my blood pressure and temperature get back to normal.'

'We'll hope that all works out well for you, then,' Abby said with a smile.

'I can't wait. I'm so looking forward to getting out of here.' Jessica hesitated. 'I had a phone call from

Daniel this afternoon,' she said, looking quietly pleased. 'He says he's going to try to get back for a visit. I really would like to be at home by then.'

'I wondered if he would get in touch,' Abby said. 'He told me he might be able to get home every now and then for a short break, and he'll have every reason to make it sooner rather than later, won't he? You shouldn't worry about being in hospital when he gets back. It won't matter to Daniel, apart from being concerned about you, and it will cheer you up to see him, won't it?'

They talked for a while longer and then, when the nurse called the end of visiting time, they said goodbye and Abby and Chloe set off for home again.

The light was beginning to fade when they returned to the house, and Chloe had fallen asleep in her seat in the back of the car. Abby lifted her out and carried her into the house, looking around cautiously to make sure that no one was lurking in the shadows.

It was probably foolish, but she couldn't get it out of her head that Richard might turn up one day when she was least expecting it. His e-mail message and the flowers had appeared innocent enough, but they could simply be camouflage. It was dangerous to be complacent where he was concerned.

She hurried inside the house, and quickly put Chloe to bed. Going downstairs a short time later, she wished that Jordan was here with her. That day, in her kitchen, when he had come to see her, his calm presence and his strength had been enough to chase away her jitters. With him by her side, nothing would bother her, she was sure.

He wasn't here, though, and she was tired of feeling afraid all the time. Perhaps she should have one last go at clearing up this whole situation, she decided. She would phone Richard and tell him she didn't want him contacting her ever again.

She dialled his number, but only got the 'unobtainable' tone. She sighed heavily. Wasn't that typical of him?

Nothing untoward happened that night, though, to her immense relief, and next morning Abby was ready to set off for work once more in a cheerful frame of mind. She left Chloe with Corinne and drove along the coast road, enjoying the glimpses of wide sandy bays lapped by a clear blue sea and bathed in morning sunshine.

Turning the car inland, she headed towards the hospital. The traffic was not too heavy at this time of day, before the morning rush hour, and as she glanced in the mirror, ready to overtake a slow-moving car hauling a caravan in front of her, she noticed a silver saloon close behind her.

She frowned. Hadn't she seen that car earlier, following the coast road, just as she had done? Hadn't the same car kept pace with her at every turn?

She flicked a second glance at it. It seemed familiar, very much like the one that Richard used to drive in London. The driver's face was in shadow, and she tried to read the number plate, but the order of the lettering was reversed by the mirror and was difficult to make out while she was trying to concentrate on the road ahead. Even so, she thought she recognised some of the digits.

Could it be Richard following her? Her heart began to thump heavily. Maybe the strain of the last few weeks was getting to her, and her mind was playing tricks on her. Even so, the thudding against her rib cage became stronger, and her breathing quickened.

She risked another glance at the driver, and saw dark hair, cut short, the face indistinct behind dark glasses, but from what she could make out, the casual jacket looked similar to one that he used to wear.

Suddenly, she made up her mind to evade him, whoever he was. Checking that the road ahead was reasonably clear, she pulled out to overtake the caravan, then shot past it, put her foot down on the accelerator and sped away. As she drove rapidly onwards, oncoming traffic stopped the silver saloon from following.

Relieved that he was being held up, Abby came to a junction and swiftly turned the car in the opposite direction from that which led to the hospital. If it was Richard, she didn't want him following her and turning up at the hospital to cause trouble.

There was a lay-by some distance away, where another car was already parked—at least she would not be alone if he turned up here—and she pulled into it, only noticing at the last minute that there was broken glass and debris alongside the grass verge.

She cut the engine and sat there until she had her breathing under control once more. Her mobile phone lay on the seat beside her, and she thought longingly of ringing Jordan, just to hear his voice.

But what could she say? He would find it hard to believe that she had got herself all hot and bothered over something that was probably nothing.

She turned and watched, surreptitiously, as Richard's car—if it was Richard—emerged at the junction and turned onto the road leading to the hospital.

Abby let out a relieved sigh. Whoever it was, he was not coming after her. When she was a little calmer, she looked around and fumbled for the car door. She was hot and uncomfortable, and her pulse was racing. Slowly she opened the door and swung her legs down on to the tarmac. A little shakily, she stood up and gulped in the cool morning air, and rubbed her clammy hands along her skirt while she tried to think about what she should do next.

A man was sitting in his car, facing outwards, the driver's door open as though he, too, wanted some fresh air. He looked up as she walked by, and muttered, 'Are you all right?' His voice was faintly uneven, as though something was wrong, but he persisted, 'You look a bit shaken up.'

'I'm fine, thanks.' She looked at the man more closely, and saw him bend his head, biting his lip as though he was in pain. 'What about you? You don't look too good yourself.' In fact, he looked as though he was about to pass out.

'Had to stop for a minute,' he said carefully. 'I'll be all right soon.'

Abby could see that beads of perspiration had broken out on his brow, and he looked as though he was about to be sick.

'You look ill,' she said. 'Could it be something that you've eaten? Perhaps you have a stomach bug.'

The man shook his head. 'Don't think so. It's nothing like what I've had before. Well, not as bad as this, anyway.' Suddenly, he doubled up and she could see that he was in real pain.

'I'm a doctor,' Abby told him. 'Abby Curtis. I work at the hospital near here. Can I help? Tell me exactly where the pain is.'

He indicated the back and the side of his body between his lower rib and his pelvis. 'Simon Langley...' he managed. 'I was on my way to work, but it got to be too much.'

'How long have you had the pain?'

'It started a few days ago. Been getting worse.' He gritted his teeth and closed his eyes as another spasm of pain hit him. 'It's there all the while,' he managed, 'and then suddenly it gets really bad.'

Abby questioned him some more, then said, 'I can give you some painkillers if you like, and then I think you need to go to hospital to get this checked out. I work in the emergency department so I can phone to let them know we're coming.'

Simon nodded, looking white-faced, as though by now the pain was intolerable. Beads of sweat were breaking out on his upper lip.

Quickly, Abby went to get her medical bag and returned to inject him with the painkiller. 'Let's see if we can get you to my car. The hospital's only a short drive from here.'

'Your tyre's flat,' he managed. 'I saw it happen when you drove up.'

Abby turned to look, and saw that he was right. In her hurry to get away from Richard, she had driven over the rubbish by the verge and now, as she inspected the damage, she could see that a nail had gone straight through the tyre.

She sucked in a quick breath. Frowning, she said in a low voice, 'I didn't see it until it was too late. I don't have time to change the tyre now—we need to get you to hospital.'

'You could drive mine.'

She nodded. 'OK.' She helped him to the passenger

seat and once he was settled and she had locked up her own car, she got out her mobile phone and called the hospital.

Jordan came to take her call, and his deep, steady tone soothed her instantly. 'What is it Abby? Are you stuck somewhere?'

'No, I'm bringing a patient in. He has symptoms of renal colic, and I'm worried about his condition. He's in a lot of pain, and I'm afraid that his condition might deteriorate rapidly if he isn't seen right away.'

'We'll be ready for you,' Jordan said. 'Just stay calm, and make sure that you drive carefully—for your sake, as well as his.'

'I will.'

She got into the driving seat of Simon's car, and set off towards the hospital. After a few minutes the painkiller began to do its job, and Simon perked up enough to ask, 'What's wrong with me? Do you know?'

'It could be a number of things,' she told him. 'We'll have to do tests to find out, but I'm working on the possibility that you have a kidney stone of some sort. You'll be asked to give a urine sample and blood for examination, and you may need to have a special type of X-ray to find out if there's any kind of blockage.'

Jordan and Sarah were waiting for them as he had promised, and Simon was quickly transferred to a trolley and taken inside. Abby was more than comforted to see Jordan. He was steadfastly in control, self-possessed and unflappable, and she felt all her troubles fade away while he was near. He had a wonderfully calming influence on her.

Jordan examined Simon then Sarah made him as

comfortable as was possible and organised a urine test. She came back to Abby and Jordan a short time later and said, 'He had some difficulty passing urine, but he did manage to give me a small sample. It's alkaline.'

Jordan turned to Abby. 'You said you thought it might be a kidney stone, didn't you? It looks as though you could be right.'

'I think we should find out where the blockage is,' Abby murmured. 'He hasn't had anything to drink for a few hours, so we could do that fairly soon.'

'That sounds reasonable.'

She explained to Simon what they were planning to do, and then he was injected with an iodine-based contrast medium. X-rays would be taken at intervals, and they should indicate the site of any blockage.

Some time later, they had a result, and Abby went to explain to Simon what they had learned.

'We think you have what is called a staghorn calculus,' she told him. 'It's a stone that forms in the kidney as the result of a bacterial infection.'

'What can you do about it?' he asked. 'I heard that these days you can blast stones with shock waves to break them up.'

'Sometimes we can. But not in your case, I'm afraid. The stone is too big, and it will have to be removed surgically. We'll need you to sign a consent form for that.'

He nodded. 'OK.' Despite the pain killing injection she had given him earlier, he was still clearly uncomfortable and finding it hard to sit still. 'When will you do it?'

'I'll call the surgeon now, and he'll add you to this morning's list.'

'I should be glad you happened to be around this morning, shouldn't I?' Simon said wanly. 'Thanks, Doc. I'm grateful for everything you've done.'

She patted his shoulder. 'My pleasure. Is there anything else I can do for you? Do you want me to contact your family?'

'Would you call my wife? Let her know that I'm OK.'

'I will. You rest easy now. The anaesthetist will come and have a look at you in a while.'

He had the operation later that day, and Abby made up her mind to go and see him as soon as he came out of Recovery. She felt responsible for him after the way she had found him that morning.

'Are you heading up to the wards?' Jordan asked, catching up with her as she walked to the lift at the end of her shift.

She nodded. 'I thought I would go and see how Simon's getting on,' she told him. 'I feel that I need to do that, somehow, after the way I found him.'

'I'll come up there with you,' he said.

She gave him a questioning look. 'I didn't realise that you followed up on patients.'

'Sometimes, I do…but actually I want a word with the surgeon,' he explained. 'Chris should be just about finishing off a ward round, and I want to have a talk with him about another patient of mine.'

'Oh, I see.'

Chris Johnson had already visited Simon, to check up on him after the operation, and the nurses had made him as comfortable as they could.

He was still a little groggy from the anaesthetic, but Abby stayed quietly at his bedside until he felt like talking.

'How are you feeling?' she asked.

'Sore,' he muttered, 'but not as bad as I felt a few minutes ago. They've given me an injection for the pain, and they said I can have painkilling tablets later.'

'The surgeon removed the stone, and everything went well, by all accounts,' Abby said.

He gave her a washed-out smile. 'At least I'm in better shape now, so my wife won't be too upset when she comes to see me.'

Abby was relieved that he was on the mend. 'You take care,' she told him. 'I'm sure you'll soon be feeling much better.'

She moved away from his bedside and went to talk to one of the nurses whom she recognised from her days as a junior house officer. Jordan emerged from the office where he had been talking to Chris and smiled briefly at both of them. Then he went to Simon's bedside, and she heard him ask how he was doing.

She only vaguely heard what was being said after that, but gathered that Simon was asking about what would happen to him now that the surgery was over, wanting to know how long he would be off work. Perhaps he hadn't felt up to asking the surgeon earlier.

Jordan answered his questions, but then he began to frown and glanced her way. Abby couldn't think of anything that she had done wrong. As far as she knew, she had followed all the correct procedures.

Shrugging inwardly, she said goodbye to the nurse and made her way down to the lobby. Whatever they were talking about, it seemed as though it involved her in some way, and it didn't look as though it was good news. Jordan's lips had tightened as he had looked at her, and she felt sure he was going to take her to task about something.

She wasn't in the mood for that right now, and all she wanted was to make a quick escape. She still had to retrieve her car from the lay-by, and perhaps the best thing would be to phone for a taxi to take her there.

She was about to go outside and use her mobile when Jordan appeared at her side.

'I'm glad I caught up with you,' he said. 'You shot off so fast that I nearly missed you. Are you deliberately trying to avoid me?'

'I'm sorry.' His sharp tone confused her. 'Should I have waited for you? I didn't know how long you were going to be.'

'I want to talk to you, Abby. I've been talking to Simon and he's given me a lot to think about. I've a few questions for you, and I want some straight answers.'

She frowned. 'That sounds serious. Have I done something wrong? Am I in trouble?'

His mouth made a straight line. He said in a low voice, 'That's part of your problem, isn't it? You always assume that you've done something wrong, and you don't have the confidence to admit that there are some things you simply can't handle on your own.'

'I don't know what you mean.'

'Don't you? I think it's time you told me what really happened this morning. I wondered what you were doing driving a different car when you brought him in. Why were you in such a hurry that you swerved into a lay-by and ended up with a flat tyre? What's going on, Abby?'

CHAPTER SEVEN

ABBY stared at Jordan. 'I've no idea what you mean,' she said lightly. There was no way she wanted to tell him that she had panicked and tried to escape from someone who might or might not have been following her. He would think that her imagination had been working overtime, and she felt foolish enough as it was.

She walked towards the main entrance of the hospital, in a hurry to get outside and make her phone call. The glass doors swished open and she went out onto the paved area, heading for the relative sanctuary of the landscaped courtyard where there were bench seats and at least a modicum of privacy.

Jordan kept pace with her, his long strides more than a match for hers. 'I think you know very well what I'm talking about. You almost crashed your car this morning and you haven't said a word about it to anybody.'

'I didn't almost crash my car,' she said in a withering tone. 'I pulled up in a lay-by so that I could get some fresh air and I didn't notice that somebody had emptied a load of rubbish onto the tarmac. Perhaps someone had to make a few quick repairs to their vehicle and didn't bother about the mess they were making when they emptied their toolbox. Anyway, however it came about, I was just unfortunate, and now I have to go and change a tyre. It's no big deal, but the sooner you leave me to get on with it, the better.'

'That's not how Simon told it.'

She raised her brows. 'Simon was ill, if you remember. How on earth could he know very much about what was going on around him?'

'He was observant enough to notice that you looked as though you were in trouble,' Jordan said crisply. 'I'm not letting you slide out of this one, Abby. I want to know what's going on, and I'm not going to let it rest until you tell me.'

'Look, this is a waste of time,' Abby retorted. 'I have to get back home and collect Chloe. I wasn't in trouble. I had a puncture—that's the long and the short of it. And now I need to go and sort it out.'

'Then that's what we'll do,' he said evenly. 'I'll give you a lift and we'll go and pick up your car. I don't see how even you can make any objection to that.'

A protest was already forming on her lips, but he glowered at her and placed a hand in the small of her back, urging her towards the car park. 'Come on. You were the one who said we were wasting time.'

He was right, of course. There wasn't any reasonable way she could object to him giving her a lift. She just hoped that he wouldn't keep wearing away at the question of what had gone on this morning. She had given him a perfectly simple explanation for what had happened, and he would have to make do with it.

A few minutes later she was sitting next to him in his car and they were on their way to the lay-by.

Thankfully, her car was still exactly as she had left it. Going over to it, she opened up the door on the driver's side and dropped her bag on to the seat before going to inspect the damage once more.

'I don't know why people throw their rubbish about like this,' she muttered. 'They obviously can't realise what problems it can cause.'

Jordan didn't answer, and she turned around to see that he had taken her keys from the door and already had her boot open. He brought out her car jack and spare tyre.

'At least your spare's in good condition,' he said. He took off his jacket and tossed it in her car, then rolled back his shirtsleeves and set to work, unloosening the wheel nuts.

His arms were lightly bronzed and strong, and she watched with absorbed interest as he worked, fascinated by the interplay of muscles and tendons as he lifted off the wheel a few minutes later.

He glanced up at her, and a flush of colour ran along her cheeks at being caught staring. 'I really didn't want to involve you in all this,' she said uncertainly. 'I know how busy you are. You must have lots of things you should be doing, rather than this.'

'Just hand me the wrench and stop fretting,' he retorted. 'You can absolve yourself of any guilt by coming out for supper with me.' He must have caught her worried expression, because he added, 'You and Chloe. And then you can explain to me what you were doing travelling in the opposite direction from the hospital, even though you insist that nothing was wrong.'

She didn't answer, but it was clear that he wasn't going to give up. He was still determined to take her out, some half an hour later, when he had sorted out her car and followed her home, and Abby racked her brains for a way that she could get out of it, without appearing churlish. She definitely wasn't in the mood for an interrogation.

Then Chloe asked him, 'Why you here?' and his mouth curved in a smile.

'I thought it might be nice to take you and Abby out somewhere to eat,' he murmured, shooting a glance at Abby.

Chloe was thoroughly excited at the prospect. 'Where we going?' she asked, pulling on his trouser leg to gain his attention. He looked down at her and smiled, and she said, 'We going play place?'

He hunkered down next to her and said softly, 'Do you want to go where they have a play area so that you can bounce around and have fun?'

Chloe's eyes sparkled. 'Yes, please.'

'Then that's what we'll do…providing it's all right with Abby.' He sent Abby a questioning look.

Abby glared at him over Chloe's head. He had manoeuvred her into a position where she could hardly refuse, without upsetting the child, and he knew it. He had the look of a man who was self-satisfied and supremely confident that he was going to get his own way.

'I suppose we could do that,' she muttered. She wasn't going to let Chloe down. Her eager little face was a joy to see, and Abby wasn't about to destroy her happiness.

She also recognised that, if he hadn't been for him wanting to question her, she would have been quietly looking forward to being with Jordan in a relaxed atmosphere, away from work. Besides, for all her attempts at bravado, she didn't really want to be alone in the house this evening. She still had the feeling that Richard might turn up, and she was very wary of what he might do. Perhaps going out with Jordan would help to take her mind off things for a while.

'Good. Then that's settled. We'll go right away, shall we?'

He wasn't giving her any chance to change her mind, and within a very short time she and Chloe found themselves in the local inn. It was a warm evening, and there were tables outside, next to a grassed play area where Chloe could run about with children of her own age. The small child soon made friends, and went to explore the swings and the low-level climbing frames nearby.

Jordan chose a table where they could watch her as she played. 'What would you like to eat?' he asked Abby.

She chose lasagne and side salad for herself, and Chloe's favourite, chips and spaghetti. He went to place the order, and Abby sat and watched Chloe while she wondered what was going on in Jordan's mind. She didn't doubt for a minute that he was still intent on pursuing his earlier question.

He came back a moment later with a tray of iced drinks, and she asked him, 'How do you know about this place? Have you been here before?'

'Yes. I've been here a few times with my brother and his family,' he said. 'The children always seem to enjoy it, and the garden stays warm till fairly late in the summertime, so it's a pleasant place to eat out. The food's good, too.'

The waitress brought their meals a short time later, and Abby thanked her and then stared abstractedly at the food. Jordan's meal was a steaming hot jacket potato topped with chicken curry and next to it a substantial mixed salad.

'Perhaps you should eat it before it gets cold.' His eyes narrowed on her and he reached for the little pot of rice that the waitress had set down on the table. He offered it to her, and when she declined he spooned some of it onto his own plate.

'Are you going to tell me what happened this morning?' he asked. 'You can't go on saying that nothing was wrong.' He tasted the food appreciatively, savouring the different flavours before adding, 'Simon told me how you had come to find him at the side of the road this morning. He said you appeared to be in a bit of a state, as though you had come there to try to get away from something.'

'He must have been mistaken.' Abby speared her lasagne with her fork and toyed with the creamy topping.

'I don't believe that.' Jordan looked at her directly. 'He said he felt that you might need protecting from something and he was worried that in his condition he might not have been able to help you if anything out of the ordinary happened. He had his mobile phone with him, and he thought the only thing he might be able to do was ring for the police. He felt bad about that.'

She made a face. 'He was in pain. He was probably not seeing the situation in its proper light. It's understandable if he made a mistake.'

Jordan shook his head. 'You're avoiding the issue, Abby, but I'm not going to be fobbed off...not this time. I'm serious about this. There have been too many instances that don't quite add up lately, and I want to know what's going on.'

'Nothing's going on.' Stoically, she tackled her lasagne. If she carried on as normal, as though nothing was out of the ordinary, he might accept that he was getting things wrong.

'Then what were you doing, going in the opposite direction to the hospital?' He tucked into the jacket potato while he waited for her to answer.

She opened her mouth to say something, and then closed it again. Chloe came up to them and Abby persuaded her to eat a little before she ran off to join her new friends once more.

Jordan ploughed on, 'I saw the way your car was parked. There's no way you could have been coming towards the hospital from that direction. He's telling me the truth. You were running away from something, and you were afraid.'

His blue-grey eyes homed in on her, caught her like a moth held in a blaze of light. 'It's time for you to start telling me the truth, Abby, before this goes too far and begins to affect your work.'

Her mouth made a rueful grimace. It always came down to her work, didn't it? He was her boss, and he needed to make sure that his team was efficient and capable, working at full capacity. What else might she have expected? That he was doing all this out of a simple rush of warm, friendly feeling? But wouldn't she have spurned him even more if that had been the case?

She had made a mistake with Richard, letting him get under her skin, and now she was paying the price for that. Jordan was right when he said she was avoiding the issue. She wanted to keep her defences intact, to be able to rely on her own powers of self-protection, and that meant that she had to stop herself from getting involved closely with anyone.

'I can handle any difficulties that I might have,' she said quietly. 'I can do it on my own, and I won't let anything affect my work. You don't need to worry about that.'

'Abby, I want to help you. I'm not here to judge you or to make things even more difficult for you. You have this shell around you that keeps people out and I don't think it's doing you any good at all. Sooner or later, something's going to give way, and I don't want to see you getting hurt.' His gaze rested on her steadily. 'I'm not giving up. I'm not going to let you try to convince me that nothing's wrong.'

She gave up all pretence of eating. Resting her hand on the table beside her plate, she said quietly, 'What makes you think that you could do anything at all to put things right?'

'Perhaps I can't,' he said soberly. 'I can only offer to try to help out.' He laid his hand over hers, and she absorbed the warmth of his palm and the gentle strength of his fingers. It was a comforting sensation, as though her whole being was flooded with the re-assurance that he was offering. Part of her longed to be able to accept it for what it was, while all the time a cool little voice inside her head was urging caution.

He said slowly, 'Whatever it is, I can be there to support you, to try to help you through it. Knowing that you're not alone is surely half the battle?'

'Maybe.' He wasn't letting go of her hand, and the intimacy of that gesture was compelling. Could she allow herself to trust him? For all his blunt manner, he was well respected by his colleagues, and she knew that he was good at his job and that he treated his patients with kindness and compassion. He never made rash promises or said that he could work miracles. He was always gently but firmly in control, and people knew that he was a man to be relied on.

'Tell me,' he said. 'What was bothering you this morning? What were you afraid of?'

She pulled in a deep breath, and said huskily, 'I thought I was being followed. It may just have been my imagination, but I saw a car behind me, and I had the feeling that it had been with me almost from the moment I left home.'

'Have you any idea who it might have been?'

She nodded. 'Someone I knew in London…an ex-boyfriend.'

'And that frightened you? Is this person dangerous?'

'He could be, I think. He doesn't like to be thwarted. He became very possessive. So possessive that one day he tried to stop me leaving his flat. I told him that I had to go, that I needed to be somewhere else, but he wouldn't listen to reason. He pushed me back against a wall and I thought he was going to hit me. Then later, after I had talked to him and tried to calm him down, I tried to leave again, but he became aggressive again and barred the way and physically held me back.'

She stopped, pulling in a shuddery breath. 'It was only because a neighbour heard me shout out and came to intervene that I managed to get away. A day or so after that, the neighbour ended up in hospital with a broken arm. He said that Richard had attacked him, but when he tried to bring charges he was told it couldn't be proved. It was his word against Richard's.'

Jordan frowned. 'Is this the same man who e-mailed you and sent you flowers?'

'Yes. I ended the relationship, but he wouldn't accept that and he made a nuisance of himself. He wasn't happy when he found out that I left London to come here. I heard that he went and caused a scene at my flat and had to be asked to leave the building.'

Abby hesitated, biting her lip. 'I may be getting this all out of proportion, of course, and he may not have been the one who was following me. I can't be sure of anything. After all, he may not even be in Cornwall.'

'But you think it's possible that he could have come after you?'

'Yes. I'm just not clear about how he got to know where I'm working or what he hopes to achieve by coming after me when I made it clear to him that it was all over between us.'

She looked up at Jordan. 'You see why I didn't want to say anything to anyone? In itself, there is nothing for anyone to be concerned about. Nothing has happened and people might think I'm simply imagining things. I thought you might be scornful.'

Jordan gently squeezed her hand. 'I'm sorry you felt that way.' His blue-grey eyes were compassionate. 'I don't think you're imagining it at all. You're intelligent and sensible, and not given to flights of fancy. I believe you.'

Relief washed over her. 'It's just that I feel so threatened somehow. It's not anything I can put my finger on, it's just there, in the background the whole time, making me nervous.'

'It's enough that you feel threatened. Sometimes our instincts are our best ally.' He paused and looked at her directly. 'Do you think he might have been the one who broke into your house?'

She nodded cautiously. 'I'm beginning to think that it might have been him all the time. Perhaps he went to Jessica's house by mistake, to begin with.' A line indented her brow. 'I suppose it could explain how he knows my e-mail address and my workplace.'

'Have you told the police about any of this?'

She shook her head. 'There's no point. They can't do anything unless he makes threats or harms me in some way, and he hasn't done that…not since I left London, and not in a way that I can prove.'

Jordan was thoughtful for a moment or two, then said carefully, 'I think the answer is for you to come and stay with me for a while. You'll feel safer having someone close by, and there's less chance that he will know where to look for you if you're at my house.'

His solution startled her. When she had recovered from the shock, she said faintly, 'You're not serious?'

'I am, very serious. You're being upset by all of this, and I want to help. Having you stay at my house is the best way I know of keeping you safe.'

The thought of living with Jordan sent a hot tingle of sensation running through her veins. What would it be like to have him close at hand the whole time… to see him at breakfast, to be near him every evening, to sleep in a room next to him? Her thoughts began to whirl out of control.

She shook her head, trying to think clearly. 'Thanks, but I can't do that.' She looked up at him, her heart filled with warmth because he had made the offer. 'Anyway, I don't want to get you any more deeply involved in this. You would just be putting yourself in the firing line, and it's my problem, not yours. It's something that I have to handle by myself. I only told you because you insisted on knowing what was going on.'

'I'm prepared for what might happen. I think it's best if I know that you're close by and I can be there if you need me. I don't want you worrying unduly.'

Abby ran her thumb gently over his hand in a gesture of affection. 'No. Thank you, but no. I can't possibly come and live with you.' She attempted a smile. 'For a start, people will talk and, second, I have Chloe to look after.'

'She could come with you,' he murmured agreeably. 'As to people talking…let them. I've absolutely nothing to hide, and I'm perfectly happy to explain the situation to them.'

She gave a wry smile. 'You're braver than I am, then. If I were a consultant, I don't think I'd be happy to have people pointing a finger at me and wondering about my private life.'

His mouth quirked attractively. 'That's why you should leave the worrying to me.' He looked at her quizzically. 'Are you going to see sense? You'll come and move in with me?'

'No way,' she said firmly. 'Anyway, Chloe needs to be in familiar surroundings. She's finding it difficult enough to cope as it is, with her mother in hospital. And when Jessica comes home, she'll need me to be there to support her. Besides, I promised my brother that I would keep an eye on his house while he's away. I can hardly do that properly if I move out.'

'All right, if that's how you feel.' His gaze was thoughtful. 'The alternative is that I should move in with you.'

Her eyes widened. 'You will not,' she said emphatically. 'I wouldn't dream of uprooting you and dragging you into sorting out my problems. Anyway,' she added, searching for something to bolster her argument, 'my brother will be coming home soon, and there will be no need for you to be concerned.' There was no need for Jordan to know that Daniel's homecoming visit was just temporary, was there?

He looked at her sceptically. 'When is he coming home?'

'I'm not sure yet, but fairly soon,' she said airily. 'I told you there was no reason for you to worry.'

'I hope you're not trying to mislead me in some way,' he murmured.

She glanced at him. He was far too suspicious for her peace of mind. She said carefully, 'He phoned me and said he was planning to come back. He's worried about Jessica. He just has to sort out a few problems at work and then arrange a flight home.'

'Hmm. In the meantime, if you're adamant that you won't consider any other arrangement, we could fix up accommodation for you and Chloe at the hospital. It only need be on a short-term basis—but at least you'll be safe until your brother arrives, and it will mean that Chloe is that much nearer to her mother. We could even try to find her a place in the hospital crèche for a few days. Will you let me set that up for you?'

Abby's eyes widened. 'I hadn't thought of that solution.' She tossed the idea around in her mind for a moment or two. Chloe would be happy to be closer to her mother, and it meant that Abby could take her to visit during the day and evening. As well as that, if Richard was stalking her, a day or two of not being able to find her might be just enough to put him off. 'I suppose that would be an answer for the time being,' she conceded.

He smiled. 'That's sorted, then. I'll make a phone call to arrange it, and then we'll go and collect some of your belongings and get you moved in this evening.'

To her amazement, he had it all organised within an hour or so, and Abby and Chloe found themselves in a four-room flat within the hospital walls. Chloe ran about, excitedly exploring her surroundings.

'Look, Abby,' she said, tugging at Abby's hand to make her come and see what she had discovered. Her eyes were wide and shining. 'I got a play table and a dolly all for me. Jordan said so.'

Abby looked, and saw a child's table, specially made for creating models out of small plastic building blocks, and a sweet-faced doll that looked brand new. She glanced across the room at Jordan, a question in her eyes, and he said lightly, 'The best side of late-night shopping. I thought they might make her feel at home. She can take them with her when she goes back to her own house.'

Abby's lips parted in a gentle smile. He had thought of everything, hadn't he? 'Thank you,' she said softly. 'You've been very kind to both of us. I really do appreciate all your help.'

The flat had been set aside for A and E staff who were on call during the night, and Abby suspected that it was meant for Jordan's own use. Since he never actually stayed there, the rooms were readily available.

Jordan helped them to settle in, and it was late when he finally prepared to leave for his own home.

'Will you be all right here?'

'I'm sure we will. Thanks, Jordan. You've been really good to me.' She reached up and hugged him, and his arms tightened around her.

'I'm glad to help.'

He lowered his head and kissed her gently and Abby felt the thrill of that kiss reverberate throughout her whole being. Her soft curves meshed with his strong body, and she loved the feel of his arms around her, the pressure of his taut thighs tangling with hers. A warm, melting tide of sensation flooded her abdomen, and a tremor of awareness tightened the nubs of her breasts.

Shakily, she let her fingers explore the strong muscles of his arms, a soft sigh trembling on her lips, but then he straightened up and was still for a moment.

Reluctantly he stepped back from her. 'I'd better go,' he said, and his face was shuttered so that she had no way of knowing what he was thinking.

Abby was utterly confused. Why was he leaving her when what she wanted more than anything was for him to stay? Was he regretting the kiss? He didn't stay to let her find out. He went out into the dark night without another word and walked swiftly away.

Abby shut the door behind him. Why would Jordan stay after the way she had refused all his offers? He was helping her out of a bad situation, that was all, and the kiss had just been his way of making her feel better about accepting his help. He didn't mean anything by it and, despite his denials, he had his position to worry about, didn't he? He was a consultant after all, and she was only a junior doctor. What would people think if he had been seen here with her, within the hospital walls?

She wasn't sure how she felt about that. Disappointed? Relieved? Why was she even contemplating getting involved with someone like Jordan? She had enough problems with Richard still trying to make inroads into her life without storing up more difficulties for herself. Perhaps things were better this way.

At least she felt safe here, at the flat. She could relax for the first time in weeks, because there were people always on call a short distance away. With a faint twist to her mouth she reflected that there would also be absolutely no problem getting to work in the mornings.

They were as busy as ever in A and E a few days later. 'We've another patient coming in,' Sarah said, putting down the phone. 'She's a woman in her mid-forties, Olivia Bradshaw. She's suffering from severe abdominal pain radiating to her back and shoulders. According to the paramedics she has a rapid pulse, low blood pressure and she's vomiting. Her daughter called the ambulance.'

'I'll be ready for her.' Abby glanced at Sarah. 'Have you seen Jordan around today? I haven't seen anything of him yet.'

'He had to go to one of the other hospitals in the area...the General, I think, to meet with some of the specialists there. He's presenting a paper at a conference later in the day, as far as I know. He mentioned it some time ago. He said he might be staying overnight at the conference hotel.'

'I didn't know.'

'Oh, I'm sorry, perhaps I should have mentioned it

earlier. I keep forgetting you haven't been with us all that long.'

Abby felt a sudden, deep sense of loss. It was silly, because he was only going to be away for a day or so from the sound of things, but she realised that she was missing him all the same. She had grown used to having him around.

As soon as her patient was brought into A and E, Abby hurried to check her over. The woman was in a lot of pain, distressed and sweating.

'I'm going to give you an injection for the pain, Olivia,' she told her as soon as she had finished her examination, 'and something to stop you from being sick.'

To Sarah, she added, 'Let her lie in the position she feels most comfortable. We'll do blood tests and an abdominal film, and we'll need to monitor her pulse, blood pressure and urine output. I'll put in a nasogastric tube and we'll give her oxygen and IV saline.'

She worked quickly, with Sarah assisting, and when she had done all that she could for the moment, she went over to the desk to glance through her charts.

A dark-haired girl, around twenty-five years old, approached her. 'Can you tell me what's wrong with my mother—Mrs Bradshaw? The paramedics and the nurse haven't been able to tell me very much. Is it serious?'

'She's in a bad way at the moment,' Abby told her, 'but it's too soon to say exactly what's wrong with her. We're trying to make her feel more comfortable, but we need to do tests to find out what's causing her problems. Perhaps you could help by giving us some idea of your mother's past history. Is there anything you can think of that might have brought on this episode? I don't have her GP's notes, so I'm working in the dark here.'

'She doesn't go to the doctor very much. She's always been stoical—and a hard worker. She reckons people should be strong and not trouble their GPs with minor ailments.' She frowned. 'These last few months, though, she's had a lot of aches and pains, some of them really bad, and I've tried to persuade her to go and see someone about them, but she wouldn't listen.'

'I'm afraid I don't think this is a minor ailment,' Abby said flatly. 'Your mother is very ill.' She paused, then asked, 'Does she drink alcohol?'

The woman shook her head. 'No, definitely not. She was never much of a drinker. She always said it disagreed with her. Why? Do you think her illness has something to do with alcohol?'

'As I said, I can't be sure yet. I'm just trying to eliminate possibilities at this stage, but it looks as though your mother could be suffering from acute pancreatitis. That's an inflammation that can bring on the type of symptoms your mother has. We need to find out what's causing the inflammation.'

Sarah was monitoring Olivia's condition closely, but some time later, as Abby was tending to a sprained wrist, she hurried over and said in a low, urgent tone, 'Abby, will you come and look at Mrs Bradshaw? She seems to be deteriorating fast. She's started to bleed out from her blood test sites—and there are bruises appearing on her skin.'

Abby handed her patient over to Nicole and rushed to Olivia's side. The woman looked desperately ill, and Abby examined her and said quickly, 'I think she's bleeding internally. Let's build up the fluids and replace the coagulation factors to try to stem the hae-morrhage. We'll keep on with the oxygen as well. Have the results come back from the lab yet?'

Sarah shook her head. 'Not yet. I'll give them an-other call to try to hurry them up.'

'Yes, do that, please. We need those results fast. There's only so much we can do for her without knowing the underlying cause of her problem.'

'We need some senior back-up here, don't we?'

Abby nodded. 'I wish that I could talk to Jordan and get his advice.' Her patient was gravely ill, and there must be something more that she could be doing for her. The senior doctor who was in charge while Jordan was away was dealing with a major emergency and she didn't want to distract him from that just yet.

Yet she was sure that Jordan would know what to do. He was miles away, though, and how could she talk to him and explain the situation properly when he was in another hospital? A phone call didn't seem to be enough.

'You could try the video link,' Sarah suggested. 'You can contact the various hospitals in the region that way. If he's available, that is…'

'Thanks, Sarah, that's a good idea. I'll give it a try.'

It was a chance worth taking. If he wasn't in con-ference at that moment, Jordan might be able to talk to her via the link, as well as see Olivia's condition for himself through a monitor.

Quickly, she set up the link and dialled the number of the hospital where he was in conference. He was tracked down with little delay.

'What's the problem, Abby?'

Relief flooded through her when she saw his image on the screen in front of her. He looked calm as usual, and simply seeing him was enough to restore her composure.

'I'm so glad I was able to reach you. I didn't know whether you would still be in a meeting and not able to talk to me.'

'We're taking a break.' He smiled. 'What's wrong?'

'My patient was brought in with symptoms of pancreatitis, but now she's taken a turn for the worse. She's bleeding internally and I don't have the test results back yet. There are a few stones in her kidneys and gall bladder, but they are small and I don't believe they would have caused this amount of damage.' She moved to allow him to see her patient for himself.

'Tell me what you've done so far.'

She told him and he nodded.

'I can see that you're giving her fluids, saline and plasma…'

'Yes, and anticoagulation factors. What more should I be doing?'

'You're doing all that you can for the moment, from the look of things. Get onto the lab again. If you discover that she's hypercalcaemic, treat for the excess calcium in the blood. You could do an ultrasound scan to check the parathyroids. There may be an adenoma that could be causing the parathyroid glands to overproduce. In that case, she'll need an operation to remove the tumour, but her condition needs to be stabilised first.'

'Thanks. I'll do that.' Abby hesitated. 'I'm sorry I had to call you in the middle of your conference.'

'Don't worry about it. I'm here to help, any time.'

Jordan broke the link a moment or two later, and Abby reflected that it had been good to see him and talk to him, even if he wasn't there in the flesh. He had been so warm and friendly, and that was what she liked so much about him. He was always there for her, wasn't he? He was supportive at work, and he was there for her in her personal life. She could get used to that. It was a good feeling, having him around. If only…

'Abby, I've got the lab on the phone.' Sarah interrupted her musings. 'Do you want to have a word with the pathologist?'

Abruptly, Abby turned away from the monitor. 'Yes, I do, thanks.' She walked quickly to take the call.

What was she doing, letting herself get all dreamy over Jordan and allowing such far-away thoughts to enter her head? It wouldn't do to start thinking wistfully about him. There was no point in it, was there? He was willing enough to help her with her problems, but as to anything else, he was way out of her league.

And anyway, her instincts were all over the place where men were concerned…her fingers had been burned once before, hadn't they?

If she had been thinking clearly she would never have got involved with Richard, and by now she ought to have learned her lesson. Hadn't Richard seemed like the ideal man to her at the start?

CHAPTER EIGHT

JORDAN walked into A and E just before Abby's shift was due to end, and she looked at him with a mixture of surprise and relief, her spirits lifting.

'I hadn't expected to see you back here today,' she said, going over to him. 'I'd heard that you were probably staying overnight at the conference hotel.'

'I wanted to see how things were with you. You looked so anxious when you called me. I thought you might need my help.'

She looked at him uncertainly. 'I didn't mean to drag you away from your meeting.'

'I know you didn't.' He smiled briefly. 'But I wanted to be here. Anyway, I need to know what's going on in my own department. I'm accountable for what happens, even when I'm not here, and when you called and told me what was happening, I decided I should come back as soon as possible.'

Disappointment washed through her veins. For a moment she had thought he might have come back to see her, and that had been a glorious feeling, but now he was telling her it was simply the department he was concerned about.

Why did that bother her so much?

'Shall we go to my office?' he said, leading the way. 'Tell me how your patient is. Has there been any improvement?'

Abby nodded. 'I think the bleeding is beginning to come under control now, and she's stable for the time

133

being. I was really worried to begin with. I didn't
know what to do, and I felt as though I was out of
my depth. It was such a relief to be able to talk to
you on the video link.'

He held the door open for her and ushered her inside the room. 'You were never out of your depth,'
he murmured. 'You were concerned for your patient,
and you were afraid that she was going to die. It's
never easy for a doctor to accept that.'

She turned to face him. 'People say that you get
used to it in time, but I don't think I ever will. I felt
sure there must be something more that I could do
for her.'

'You did what you could.' He put his hands on her
shoulders and his thumbs gently kneaded her skin in
a gesture of reassurance. She felt the warmth of his
fingers seep through her thin cotton top, and wondered why it was that he could make her feel so feminine and vulnerable…and at the same time cloud her
head with the notion that there was something missing
in her life.

'You did everything possible,' he murmured, 'and
you shouldn't blame yourself if it doesn't seem to be
enough. It's a sad fact, but when someone is as ill as
your patient, there's more than a twenty per cent
chance that they could die. It's hard for us to come
to terms with that. Don't you think everyone would
feel as desperate as you did in those circumstances?'

'I don't know. It's hard for me. I don't have the
experience…'

'You're a good doctor, Abby,' he said softly. 'Have
faith in yourself. I have faith in you.'

'Do you?' She looked at him doubtfully and he
smiled gently, bending his head towards her so that

his lips brushed hers and tested the softness of her mouth.

'I do,' he said huskily, looking into her eyes. Still unsure of herself, she met his gaze a little shakily, her lips parting, still registering the imprint of his. His arms closed around her, drawing her to him, and she slowly absorbed his strength, aware of the irresistible feeling of happiness that stirred in her whenever he was close by. More than anything, she wanted to respond, but even now something held her back.

He could make her senses erupt in chaos just by touching her, and she didn't know how she would cope if he wanted more and then it all ended in chaos and disillusion.

His hand stroked along the small of her back, triggering a meltdown of all her defences. 'It's all right, Abby,' he murmured. He kissed her again, and her pulses raced, the blood running hotly through her veins.

Tentatively, she returned his kiss, tantalised by the way his lips pressured hers, the way his hands caressed and explored her feminine curves. Bubbles of excitement fizzed inside her, making her mind swim with heady sensation.

The distant sound of a trolley clattering along a corridor brought her back to reality with a jolt. What was she doing? Trembling, she put a hand to his chest, the palm flat against his rib cage, and she felt the heavy thud of his heartbeat beneath her fingers.

He drew back, looking into her troubled eyes. He gave a faint grimace and said quietly, 'I shouldn't have done that. I'm sorry. I'm not sure why it happened. I can't have been thinking straight.'

He withdrew his hands from her and moved away,

and she felt a chill of isolation sweep over her all at once. She knew well enough why it had happened. He had kissed her because he had seen her vulnerability, and he had wanted to comfort her, to soothe away her distress, but she should never have let him do that, should she? She wasn't ready for any of this.

'Did you get the results back from the lab?' he asked, and his tone was once more brisk and businesslike.

She nodded slowly, trying to gather her thoughts. 'I did, eventually. There is too much calcium in her blood, and that led to inflammation and a variety of symptoms. Then she went into shock and the bleeding started. I haven't come across that before.'

'What happens is that the coagulation process is triggered, and the platelets and coagulation factors are used and broken up faster than they can be replaced by the liver. That can result in severe bleeding.' He sent her a swift glance. 'Did you investigate the causes of the hypercalcaemia?'

She nodded, relieved that she was beginning to regain her composure. 'I did. I suspect her parathyroid glands have been over-active, as you suggested, and from the scan it looks as though there might be a small tumour. I've consulted with Mr Johnson, and he's going to operate.'

'Good. Let's hope he can resolve the problem, for her sake.'

'I hope so, too. She's relatively young, and she has a family who need her. It would be tragic if anything more went wrong.'

Awkwardly, she moved towards the office door. 'I should go now. I have to collect Chloe from the crèche.'

'Shall I come and see you at the flat later? You seem to have settled in all right. Is there anything you need?'

She shook her head. 'No, thank you, there's nothing I need. Actually...' She hesitated, then said, 'We're moving back to the house tonight.'

He frowned. 'Why is that? I thought things were working out for you here?'

'They are...but my brother is arriving home this evening, and I want to go and see him and make sure that everything is ready for him. It's worked out well, with the weekend coming up and my off-duty time coinciding.' She paused, thinking about the things she needed to organise. 'I expect he'll want to go and see Jessica later, and he might even be able to bring her home with him.'

'She's feeling better, then?'

'Much better. The infection seems to have cleared up. Her blood tests show that her haemoglobin level is back to normal, and the ulceration seems to have settled down. If we can keep her stress-free, we should be able to prevent this sort of thing happening again.'

'That's probably easier said than done.'

'Yes...well, at least my brother will be able to help out there.'

Jordan nodded. 'Just remember that the flat is there for you whenever you need it.'

'I will.'

She went straight home from the hospital, having picked up Chloe from the crèche. 'We go see Mummy?' Chloe asked excitedly.

'Yes, sweetheart. We'll go and meet Daniel at the airport first, and then we'll all go together to see your mummy.'

Daniel greeted them both with a hug. Tall, with dark, flyaway hair, he looked bronzed and fit, and Abby was glad to see him again.

He kissed her warmly on the cheek, and then turned to Chloe. 'I've missed you,' he told the little girl. 'I was thinking about you a lot while I was in South America, and I brought a present back with me just for you.'

Chloe's eyes were sparkling with excitement. 'What is it?'

'You'll see,' he said, and they waited for his luggage to arrive. Apart from his suitcases, there was a huge parcel, wrapped in brown paper and tied with string, and Chloe stared at it, her mouth dropping open, her eyes growing bigger by the moment.

'That for me?' she asked, as Daniel held it out to her. It was bigger than she was, and when Daniel nodded, she scrambled to unwrap the paper.

'Here, let me help.' Daniel gave a hand tugging at the wrapping, and a few seconds later Chloe was cuddling a fleecy sloth cuddly toy.

She buried her face in his soft fur and said contentedly, 'I love him…I love him.'

Abby smiled. 'He's going to take up a seat and a half in the car,' she murmured.

'That's nothing. You should have seen the trouble I had getting him through customs.' Daniel laughed. 'Some very odd looks came my way until he went through the X-ray machine. Still, it was worth it, just to see her smile.'

They walked to Abby's car and he asked, 'How is

Jessica? You said she was on the mend now. Is that true? I was really worried when you told me what had happened.'

'She's a lot better. We should be able to take her home with us, if the doctor gives her the all-clear.'

They arrived at the hospital a couple of hours later, and the doctor was just finishing off a ward round.

'She can go home,' he said, 'as long as she takes things easy for the next few weeks.'

'We'll make sure that she does,' Daniel promised.

He put his arm around Jessica and held her close. 'I'm going to put in for a different job,' he told her. 'One that means I can stay in the UK and be with you.'

'Really? You mean it?' Jessica looked at him in pleased surprise.

He nodded. 'It will take a while to sort out, but I've a couple of offers to consider.'

They went home and had supper together at Jessica's house. Later, Jessica insisted that she was well enough to take Chloe up to bed.

'I want to go with her and see her tucked in,' she said. 'It's one of the things I've really missed, being in hospital.'

Chloe held onto her new fleecy toy, insisting that he sleep next to her in the bed.

Abby watched them go upstairs, and then went into the kitchen to make coffee.

Daniel said quietly, 'You said the Social Services people were trying to contact Jessica's parents. Has there been any news?'

Abby shook her head. 'I think they have an address, but her parents are away on holiday and no one has been able to reach them.'

'I think I'll try to get in touch with them,' Daniel said. 'This rift has gone on long enough and Jessica needs to have her family round her. She's too stubborn, or proud, to do it herself, but I can't believe that they don't want to know her.'

'I hope it all works out,' Abby said, 'but tread carefully, whatever you do. By all accounts, it hasn't been easy for her these last few years.'

'I will.'

When Abby went into work on Monday morning, there was an atmosphere of change in the department. Jordan was getting kitted up as though he was off somewhere, and a paramedic from the air ambulance team was talking to him.

'What's going on?' Abby asked.

'I'm doing a stint with the air rescue service,' Jordan told her. 'It's something we do every now and again. It helps keep us abreast of what's going on in the outside world, and gives us an idea of what the paramedics have to contend with.'

'I think I heard that something like this was going to happen,' Abby said, 'but I thought all this was scheduled for a couple of months or so from now.'

He nodded. 'It was, but we decided the weather might start to break up then, and now would be a better time. Actually, we're a man short. One of the house officers was to have come along as well, but in the end Owen had to back out at the last minute because of trouble with knee cartilage. He's in good enough shape to work at the hospital, but it wouldn't be such a great idea for him to come out with the rescue team. It's a shame, because it would have been valuable experience for him.'

She sent him a thoughtful look. 'Could I come along…in Owen's place?'

He frowned. 'Are you sure that you want to? Some of the situations can be quite tricky, given the landscape around here.'

'I'm sure. When I came in with the helicopter on the first day, it was a new experience, and I thought it was something I'd like to see more of.'

'Well…if you're certain, I can't see any reason why not. Owen will be here to cover for you.'

'Thanks.' She smiled at him warmly. 'I'll go and get ready, shall I?'

They went out on their first mission a couple of hours later. 'We're heading south, to an area somewhere around Land's End,' the paramedic said.

Harry was a fair-haired man in his thirties, capable and confident. 'A young lad has fallen on the rocks. His name's Jack, and he's fifteen years old. We don't know his condition yet, except that he's conscious and in a lot of pain. The weather conditions aren't too good today, unfortunately, and that might make things a bit difficult for us.'

There was a fine drizzle of rain in the air, and a lot of mist hanging over the coastline as they approached the area where the boy had fallen. As they came closer and hovered, Abby could see the craggy outline of a promontory, with the sea lashing at its base. The rocks would be slippery and treacherous, and the boy must have been foolhardy to go exploring in any conditions, let alone these.

A chill ran through her, and she must have been holding her breath because Jordan leaned towards her and said, 'Are you OK?'

Abby nodded, but he searched her face and asked, 'Are you having second thoughts?'

'No.'

'But you're thinking about your father?'

It was typical of him that he would home straight in on what was troubling her. She nodded again, and pulled in a deep breath. It had all happened a long time ago, but coming here like this had brought it all flooding back to her. The sadness and sense of loss was as real to her now as it had been then.

He reached for her hand and squeezed it gently. 'I know this must be hard for you. You can sit this one out, if you like. You don't have to go down there.'

'I know...but I will, if I'm needed.' She steeled herself to conquer her fear. She would not let them down by going to pieces before they had even started.

Harry was carefully lowered down to the boy, who was lying on a wide strip of rock, several feet from the land surface above. After a few minutes, he gestured that he needed help, and Jordan made the descent.

Then Abby was strapped into a harness and lowered, inch by inch, to the surface of the rock. The wind was blustery and she was thankful that she was dressed in waterproof overalls that kept the worst of the sea spray from penetrating through to her skin.

The boy was in a bad way. Jordan examined him and discovered that any movement of the boy's shoulder caused him intense pain. 'I think it's a fracture of the head of the humerus,' he told Abby. Continuing his examination, he checked the boy's legs and grimaced. 'It looks as though he has a fractured tibia as well, but I don't think the knee has been damaged too badly.'

To Jack, he said, 'We're going to give you something for the pain, Jack, and then we'll try to make you comfortable so that we can get you into the helicopter and off to hospital.'

Abby helped Jordan to splint the leg, while Harry put a collar and cuff support around the boy's arm. Then, together, working carefully on the narrow ledge, they strapped Jack to a stretcher and attached him securely to a harness so that he could be lifted up into the helicopter. Harry went back up first, so as to receive him at the other end.

Abby watched as the manoeuvre was carried out, and there was a terrifying moment when she saw Jordan almost lose his footing as he released his hold on the stretcher. She reached out to grab him and desperately tried to pull him back.

Jack was safe, but Jordan might easily have plunged into the sea below had he not recovered his balance in time. She held onto him as though she would never let him go, her breathing ragged.

'Hey, what's this?' he asked, looking into her worried eyes.

'I thought you were going to fall,' she said in a choked voice. 'I was so scared, I didn't know what to do.'

He put his arm around her and hugged her close. 'I'm fine,' he said. 'There was nothing to worry about. I was perfectly safe.'

Even so, she was relieved when they were both safely back in the helicopter once more.

Their patient was transferred quickly to hospital, where Jordan ordered X-rays.

'He'll need to have the bones manipulated into place under anaesthetic, and we'll keep him in hospital for observation for a while,' he told Jack's worried parents, who had arrived at the hospital moments after the air ambulance. 'He'll need to have his leg in plaster while it heals, and later he'll be checked at intervals in outpatient clinics. The nurse will talk to you about follow-up procedure.'

Once the parents had been taken off to a waiting room by Nicole, Jordan and Abby had a few moments' respite. Harry had gone to get himself a mug of soup and was talking to Sarah by the desk.

'That must have been a difficult experience for you, in more ways than one,' Jordan said, glancing at Abby as he poured coffees for both of them in his office. 'Perhaps it was unfortunate that a rock fall was our first casualty.'

'It was more unfortunate for Jack than it was for me,' Abby muttered, taking the mug that he offered her and sipping at the hot liquid. It warmed her through and through and comforted her.

'You said your family moved away after your father died. Did that make things any easier for you?'

'I suppose it helped us to cope at first. We went to stay with my uncle, my mother's brother. Uncle Steve could see how badly shaken my mother was, and he wanted to do whatever he could to help. She went to pieces after my father died, and he offered us a home, where she could be with her family.'

She shrugged. 'It took us away from the place that would remind us of what happened, of course, but nothing was ever quite the same again. I think that being uprooted from everything we had ever known, moving away from all our friends, didn't help.'

'But eventually, as time went on, didn't you get used to it...didn't things change for the better?'

'It was good for my mother, but Daniel and I never quite adjusted to the new life. My uncle took charge of us when my mother fell apart, and he was quite strict and liked to be in control. We weren't used to that. We had always been given a fairly free hand when our father was alive, but our uncle had his own way of looking at things and he wasn't used to dealing with rebellious teenagers.'

'He must have felt a strong sense of responsibility towards you.'

'Yes, I think he did. I don't think he knew how to handle us, though, so he tended to be restrictive and heavy with the rules about how things should be done. We reacted badly to that.'

'Perhaps you and your brother resented him taking over your father's role?'

'That's probably true.' She gave a faint smile. 'We must have made him suffer, poor man. Thankfully, we get on a lot better with him these days.'

Jordan swallowed some of his coffee and studied her over the rim of his mug. 'I imagine that going through all that must have made you wary of domineering men.'

She nodded. 'Yes, I think it did.'

He frowned. 'So why did you let yourself get involved with Richard?' He put the mug down on the table. 'Didn't you see the signs in him?'

'There weren't any. Not to begin with, at any rate. He was gentle and kind, and he did everything he could to make me happy. It was only later that the cracks started to appear and he became jealous and possessive and started to show his true nature.'

'You did the right thing, getting out of that relationship.'

'I think so, too.'

She might have said more, but Harry appeared at the office door just then, and said, 'We've had another call...a woman who's gone into labour in a remote rural area. The midwife thinks she needs to come into hospital urgently.'

'We're right with you.' Jordan was already walking to the door and Abby followed swiftly.

When they reached the woman, it was clear that she needed an emergency Caesarean in order for her and the baby to be safe.

'We'll get you to hospital within a few minutes,' Abby told her. 'The team is standing by in Theatre waiting for you. Just try to relax.'

The woman would be given an injection to anaesthetise her while the operation was performed. Abby monitored the baby's heartbeat. He was showing signs of distress, and Abby thought that the sooner the poor little thing could be brought into the world, the better.

The journey to the hospital took about ten minutes, and the baby was delivered just a short time later. He made no sound and appeared to be lifeless as the doctor lifted him away from his mother, and Abby felt her heart contract painfully.

The theatre nurse applied a suction tube to his nose and mouth and quickly cleaned him up, and after a few seconds he gave a little wail.

Abby darted a swift look at Jordan, and above the mask he was wearing she saw his eyes crinkle. She let out a sigh of relief as the nurse wrapped the baby and laid him gently in his mother's arms. The infant was going to be all right.

By the end of the day, Abby was exhausted, but

exhilarated at the same time. They were late getting back because an emergency had cropped up just as they were about to finish, and by now it was beginning to get dark.

'What did you think of your first day with the air ambulance?' Jordan asked, and she sent him a glance that was full of excited appreciation.

'I'm thrilled that I had the chance to go along with you,' she said. 'Though I shan't be sorry to get home and soak in the bath for half an hour or so.'

Jordan laughed. He was heading for the car park, and she suddenly remembered that she didn't have her car with that day.

'I'm going the wrong way,' she said. 'I need to go and order a taxi. I'm too tired to go and wait for a bus.'

'Why—where's your car?'

'Daniel borrowed it. He sold his car when he went to South America…it seemed the sensible thing to do, since Jessica doesn't drive. He was going to pick me up after work, but I rang and told him that I would be late getting back. I don't want to fetch him out at this time of the evening.'

'I'll take you home.' He took her arm and guided her towards his car.

It was a luxurious feeling, leaning back against the cushioning seat next to him. He drove smoothly, and switched on the CD player so that soft music filled the air.

'Here we are,' he said a short time later, and she blinked and looked around. 'You're home,' he murmured. 'Though if I had my way you wouldn't be staying here, you would be in the flat at the hospital where I can keep an eye on you.'

He was giving her a narrowed look, and she turned away from his scrutiny and fumbled for the door catch. She could see a light on in the house, and she guessed that Daniel was at home.

Jordan came around and helped her out of the car, and as they walked towards the front porch she said huskily, 'Would you like to come in for a coffee?'

He looked regretful. 'I can't,' he said. 'I'm already running late. I'm supposed to be meeting my parents and my brother and his family in ten minutes. It's a special anniversary and we're having a big get-together.'

'That sounds good,' she murmured, trying to shake off the quiver of disappointment that ran through her.

'I expect it will be.' They were in the shelter of the porch now, and the light from the lamp sent a golden glow around them. Jordan looked at her upturned face and lightly caressed her cheek with his finger. 'You did well today. Parts of it can't have been easy for you, but you were brilliant. I was glad you were with me.'

'Thanks.'

His arms went around her, holding her tightly, and then his mouth claimed hers and the blood rushed to her head and she felt as though the world was spinning, exhilaration fizzing inside her.

Her lips softened and parted and she gave herself up to the kiss, loving the feel of his mouth on hers, the warm protective embrace of his arms holding her close.

She could feel the strength of his hard body against her softly feminine curves as he gently pressed her into the shelter of the porch, and it was a good feeling, an enticing, bone-melting whirl of sensation. She wanted this moment to go on for ever.

Then she heard a rustling sound, a strange scuffling in the background, and her senses were suddenly on alert. She stiffened, unsure what it was that she had heard.

'What's wrong?' Jordan looked down at her, searching her face.

'Nothing. It was nothing.' Then she heard it again, faintly, almost like a breeze blowing gently through the undergrowth. But there was no breeze.

She shivered, a whisper of cold stirring her senses. Were they being watched?

'Abby?'

'I'm sorry. I… Perhaps I should go inside the house now.'

He frowned. Then he drew back and said, 'Maybe you're right. It's late and I should be going. I'll wait until you're safely inside.'

She turned and put her key in the lock and he moved away from her and went back to his car without saying anything more. She watched him get into the driver's seat and she knew that he had the wrong idea, that he thought she was turning him away, but she didn't want to tell him the truth, to worry him with her troubles, not again, not now.

She gave him a small wave, then went inside the house and closed the front door. She heard him drive away, and she felt sad, as though she had just lost something precious.

CHAPTER NINE

ABBY found Daniel upstairs at the back of the house. He was packing a suitcase ready for his flight back to South America next day, and as she watched him make preparations, she realised that she was going to miss his cheerful presence around the place.

'How long will you be away for?' she asked. She tried not to let her thoughts dwell on Jordan, or on whether or not there might have been anyone prowling about outside. The doors were locked and bolted, and Daniel was here, for the moment at least.

'About a month,' he said. 'I have to finish the project that I'm working on before I can organise things back here, but I'll try to do it all as quickly as I can.'

'Jessica will be sorry to see you go.'

'I know she will. I've told her that I'm going to finish this last bit of packing, and then I'll go round and spend some more time with her.' He paused, folding a sweater and laying it down in his suitcase. 'I'm glad that you're here to watch out for her, but I wish that I could have brought her and her parents back together again before I go. I got hold of their phone number and I've left a message on their answering-machine, but it doesn't look as though they're going to get in touch before I have to leave.'

'If they phone here after you've gone, I'll talk to them and try to explain the situation.' She looked at him with a sad expression. 'I wish that we could have

150

had longer together,' she said wistfully. 'It's been good, having you home.'

'I'll be back in a few weeks,' he said with a smile. 'We'll get together again then.' He zipped the case shut and reached for a holdall. 'You said you had been out on the air ambulance today. Will you be doing that again?'

'Yes, I'll be going out with the rescue team for the next few days. It's a whole new experience—but it's a little scary sometimes. You never know what situation you're going to end up in.'

'I can imagine that it would be unsettling. In A and E you work in familiar surroundings, don't you? That must be a help when you're faced with making difficult decisions. It's one less thing that you have to think about.'

'That's true.' Though it had helped enormously having Jordan with her on the air ambulance. She had felt safe with him, as though she could tackle anything as long as he was by her side. He was considerate, supportive and she knew she could rely on him to help her get through most things.

Would he still be the same with her after today, though? She had ruined everything by distancing herself from him, hadn't she?

She pulled herself together and watched Daniel as he stuffed essentials that he would need on the flight into his holdall. 'Do you want me to drive you to the airport after breakfast?'

'Will you have time?'

'I'm on a late shift tomorrow.'

He smiled. 'Thanks. That would be good.'

They had breakfast with Jessica and Chloe next morning, and afterwards, when it was time to leave,

Abby took the little girl into the garden for a few minutes, giving the other two a little privacy in order to say their goodbyes. She could see that Jessica was upset by the impending separation, though she tried hard to hide it for fear of distressing Chloe.

Jessica watched from the porch as Daniel loaded his luggage into the car.

'He'll be back before you know it,' Abby said, squeezing her arm.

Jessica wiped away a tear. 'I suppose so. It's just that I love him so much, and I hate being away from him. I've never known anyone like Daniel. He's kind and loving and gentle...and I shall miss him desperately. I don't know what I'm going to do without him.'

'He loves you, too. That's why he came back.' Abby smiled at her. 'Try not to get too upset. We'll have supper together tonight, if you like. We'll talk and have a think about all the things we can do to make the time go faster.'

'I'd like that.' Jessica attempted a smile. 'You're a good friend, Abby. I don't know what I'd have done without you these last few weeks.'

'I'll see you when I finish work,' Abby said. 'Go and talk to Corinne when you get back from taking Chloe to nursery school. She looks forward to your company.'

'I will.'

Abby drove to the airport a short time later, and waited until Daniel was ready to go through to the boarding lounge. 'Take care of yourself,' she said. 'Keep in touch.'

She was sad to see him go, but it was only later as she drove to the air ambulance headquarters that she realised she was now truly on her own. Now that he had gone, she would be alone in the house, and it was hard to shake off the growing feeling that, sooner or later, Richard would put in an appearance.

There was no way she could move back to the hospital flat as Jordan had suggested. She was bound to stay at the house so that she could make sure that Jessica was all right. It hadn't been long since she had come out of hospital, and she needed support.

Abby parked her car next to Jordan's at the rescue team's headquarters. There was a chill in the air this morning, and as she walked towards the building she rubbed her arms to stave off the shiver of cold that ran through her.

Jordan was speaking on the phone when she walked into the room where the team was assembled, and she gathered from his conversation that he was talking to Sarah in A and E.

'Problems?' she asked.

He looked at her and shook his head, but his expression was remote. 'I was just checking up on the boy we brought in yesterday. He's doing all right, apparently.'

He half turned and glanced at the pilot, Dave, and the paramedic and smiled. 'Well enough to want the rescue team to sign his leg plaster, anyway.' They acknowledged with a cheery lift of their mugs of tea.

Jordan wasn't including her in the camaraderie, and Abby was dismayed by the way he seemed to be distancing himself from her.

It was her own fault, she recognised that well enough, and she wished that things could be different, but deep down she was still nervous about relaxing her guard and letting someone in. The last few months while she had been trying to escape from Richard had been painful and distressing, and she was afraid to go through any more hurt and disillusion. Wasn't that exactly what would happen if she opened up her heart to Jordan?

She stiffened her shoulders and said with an effort, 'While you're on the phone, will you ask Sarah how Olivia Bradshaw's doing?'

He frowned. 'Is that the woman who was suffering from pancreatitis?'

'That's right. She was operated on yesterday afternoon—and Sarah was going to check up on her for me. There was a tumour.'

'I remember.' Jordan spoke to Sarah once more, then thanked her and put the receiver down.

'She came through the operation reasonably well,' he said in a level tone, his manner every bit as professional as it had always been. 'Her blood pressure fell alarmingly, but she pulled through, and by all accounts she's on the road to recovery.'

'And the tumour?'

'Benign. It was an adenoma that caused her parathyroid glands to become over-active.'

Abby gave a sigh of relief. 'I'm glad. I was really worried about her.'

'You can't afford to let yourself get so involved,' Jordan said curtly. 'If you grieve over every patient that way, you'll fall apart.'

Abby was stung by his remark, enough to protest sharply, 'Didn't you get involved the same way with the boy who fell on the rocks? Or am I supposed to have imagined the conversation you just had with Sarah?'

'That was different. I was simply following up on our procedures.'

She glowered at him, but held back from saying any more. She sensed that the air ambulance team had begun to show an interest in their brisk exchange and she didn't want to invite their curiosity any more than she had to.

Instead, she turned to Harry and asked, 'What's the drill for today?'

He started to outline the day-to-day routine, and a few minutes later, as she was sipping a coffee and getting ready to look over the maps of the area the rescue service covered, their first call came in. It was to a road traffic accident, and it was the beginning of a series of incidents that kept them on their toes throughout the day.

Late in the afternoon, though, they were heading back to the base, relieved that all had gone well so far, when Dave signalled that an urgent message was coming in. He listened, then said, 'OK, we're only a few miles away. We'll be there in a couple of minutes.' He turned the helicopter westwards and headed towards the coast.

'There's been a possible drowning incident,' he told them. 'It's a child, three or four years old. They've just brought him out of the water, but it's not looking good.'

Abby's heart began to pound, so heavily that it was almost painful. She was beginning to discover that she could cope with most things, but when it was a child who was in trouble, she wasn't so sure...

She glanced at Jordan, and saw that his features were closed, his mouth set in a straight line. Was he feeling the pressure, too? Timing was crucial here, and precious minutes could make a vital difference.

Perhaps it wasn't taking very long to get there, but it seemed like an age to Abby. As soon as the helicopter landed, they jumped down and ran to where a small crowd had assembled on the beach.

As Jordan reached them the people moved aside to let him through. Their faces showed their concern, the men shocked and pale, the women weeping silently.

Abby looked and saw that a lifeguard was working to save a small child, and a woman, presumably the boy's mother, was kneeling down alongside the infant, tears coursing down her cheeks. The child appeared to be lifeless.

Jordan knelt down beside the woman, and spoke quietly to her. 'What's his name?'

'Ryan,' she said in a choked voice. 'His name's Ryan. Please, tell me that you can do something for him.'

He turned to the lifeguard. 'How long was he in the water?'

'About five minutes, I'd say. He was being swept out to sea and the water was icy cold.' The lifeguard continued with cardiopulmonary resuscitation, but his features were grim. 'I've managed to get some water out of him, but there's been little response so far. I'm not getting a pulse.'

'Let me have a look at him.' Jordan made a swift examination, and frowned. 'We'll intubate and ventilate. Let's get some suction going.'

Harry took over from the exhausted lifeguard and continued with CPR while Abby put a tube in place to help drain away any excess water. Once she had done that, she struggled to put in an intravenous line. The child's circulation was closing down rapidly.

Jordan charged the paddles of the portable defibrillator and prepared to shock Ryan's heart into activity. 'Clear,' he said, and applied the paddles to the boy's chest.

There was still no heartbeat and Abby looked at Jordan in dismay.

'His core temperature is probably way down,' he said. 'He's hypothermic and the defibrillation won't work until we can get his temperature higher. For now we'll wrap him in the space blanket, give him adrenaline and keep on with the CPR.'

Ryan's mother watched their efforts, her face ashen. 'He was paddling in the sea,' she said in a voice that was barely above a whisper. 'We only looked away for a minute…' She began to sob, great gulps that stopped her from getting her words out. 'My husband was going to get ice cream. Then when I…' She pulled in a shuddery breath. 'When I looked again…Ryan… I couldn't see him. He…he wasn't there.'

'I know,' Abby said, frowning as she persevered in trying to gain access to a vein. 'These things happen so quickly.'

Jordan glanced at her. 'Can you get a line in?'

'I'm doing my best… Give me just a few more seconds… Yes…there it is.' She breathed a sigh of relief. She queried which drug to use in a low voice and Jordan confirmed it with a nod.

'Yes, let's deal with the liquid in the lungs as quickly as we can.'

As soon as they had done all they could for the child on the beach, they transferred him hastily to the helicopter, and continued CPR. The child's mother sat alongside him, not crying now but desperately holding onto his hand and talking quietly to him the whole time, even though he wasn't making any response. Her husband, shocked and uncommunicative, was going to make his way to the hospital by car.

Abby looked down at the little boy and was desperately afraid that they were too late. She had never been in this kind of situation before, and she would follow Jordan's lead. As long as he was prepared to go on fighting for the child, she would hold onto hope.

'We should call ahead and tell them to prepare for Ryan at the hospital,' Abby said worriedly, when they were airborne once more.

Jordan nodded. 'Dave's already doing that. In the meantime, we'll get these wet things off him and start to warm him up. We can use warmed oxygen and saline to warm him from the inside, and a space blanket and polythene sheets to get his temperature up externally.'

As soon as the helicopter landed, they rushed the boy into A and E, where Sarah and the rest of the team were waiting, and Jordan tried to shock his heart with a defibrillator once more.

'We've got a heartbeat,' Abby said, her voice rising. 'It's very faint, though.'

'We still need to get him warmer, or we'll lose him,' Jordan warned. 'He's not out of the woods by a long way. We can't try dialysis because his heart rhythm makes it risky.' He turned to Sarah. 'Get the surgeon down here, will you? We'll try a cardiac bypass machine.'

Harry and Dave stood about, waiting for developments, relieved that there were no other calls to distract them. 'Do you want coffee?' Nicole asked. 'You're probably in for a long wait, so you might as well go and get something to eat as well. There are biscuits in the staff kitchen.'

They shook their heads. 'Just coffee,' Dave said. 'I'll go and get it.'

Chris Johnson arrived in double quick time and got to work. Seeing Mrs Lowe's anguished expression, Jordan put an arm around her and gently guided her away from A and E.

'What are they doing to him?' the bewildered mother asked. 'Why can't I see him?'

'We're going to put him on a cardiac bypass machine,' Jordan explained gently. 'The surgeon will put tubes into Ryan's circulatory system, and then his blood will go to the bypass machine which will warm it and supply it with oxygen before returning it to his circulation. It's the best chance we have of warming him up.'

He called Nicole over, and said quietly, 'Will you take Mrs Lowe to go and get a cup of tea? Her husband should be arriving any time now. See if you can find him, will you, and let him know?'

Abby couldn't settle to anything. She tried updating her notes, going through the backlog of files that she had to put in order, but nothing took her mind off what was going on.

She began to pace the floor, waiting, praying for the infant to pull through. After a while, Jordan came over to her, and said in a low voice, 'You should have gone off duty over an hour ago.'

'Should I?' She looked at him blankly. 'I can't go anywhere. Not until I know…'

'We're doing everything that we can for him.' He turned her towards the doctors' lounge and held open the door.

She nodded. 'I know that,' she said, going into the room. 'I know that I should be strong, but it's the waiting, the not knowing...' She looked up at him, her green eyes clouded. 'Jordan, he can't be much older than Chloe. He's just a baby, really.' A sheen of tears blurred her eyes and she blinked them away. 'If I had a child, I don't think I could bear it if something like this happened to him...'

'Is that something you've thought about...having children?'

Her mouth wavered. 'Sometimes...' she whispered. 'Sometimes I wonder what it would be like to have a baby of my own...an infant to cradle, to love...' She sent him a helpless glance. 'I suppose it's being around Chloe that has brought it all into my mind lately. She's such a sweet, happy little girl, and I can't help but think what it would be like to...'

She broke off, pressing her lips together. Motherhood wasn't likely to come her way, was it? Given her present circumstances, she couldn't even think about getting involved without breaking out in a nervous sweat. Even though Jordan would make a wonderful father...

Why had that thought crept into her head, right out of the blue? Heat flooded every part of her, and she turned away, not wanting him to see, to guess what she had been thinking.

'Abby?' He had moved closer, but just then the door to the lounge was pushed open.

'The boy's coming round.' Sarah broke the news

with a wide smile. 'He's opened his eyes and he's looking around. I'll go and fetch the parents, shall I?'

Abby let out a long breath. She hadn't fully appreciated how tense she had been until that moment, and now it all came out in a great sigh of relief.

'Yes,' Jordan said. 'Take them to see him. I'm sure he'll want to be with his family.'

Sarah went out and shut the door, and Abby looked up at Jordan. His mouth had gentled into a smile and she wanted to reach up and touch him, to run her fingers along his cheek, to hold him close.

Instead, she said quietly, 'I wasn't sure that it would work. I didn't think anyone could survive when they had been brought out of the water in the state he was.'

'It's a kind of diving reflex that can save a child's life under certain circumstances,' Jordan murmured, 'but it depends on a number of factors. If he had been submerged for longer than a few minutes, the outcome might have been very different, and the temperature of the water is important, too. If it's very cold it can cause a lowered heart rate and lowered metabolic demand. That helps to stop the damage that lack of oxygen to the brain would normally cause.' He gave a wry smile. 'In a way, he's a very lucky boy.'

'It was lucky for him and his parents that you were there soon after it happened,' Abby said. 'You knew what to do for him. It was your skill and knowledge that saved him.'

'No,' he said, gazing down at her upturned face. 'It was teamwork that saved his life.' He put his arms around her and drew her close, and Abby felt warm and safe for the first time in a long while. 'It was a combination of united effort and circumstances. The lifeguard was there at the right time, the rescue service was on hand when it was needed…and the team here at the hospital went into action as soon as we arrived.'

'Maybe…but I still think that you were terrific out there.' It felt good to be locked in his arms, to feel the satisfying rise and fall of his chest beneath her cheek, the steady thud of his heart sounding in her ear. If only he could always be there for her, nothing in the world would ever hurt her again. How could anything compare with simply being with the man she loved?

Abby drew in a sharp breath, suddenly realising where her dreamy thoughts had taken her. Love…that was it. She loved him, every bit as much as Jessica loved Daniel.

He must have heard the intake of breath, because he eased away from her slightly so that he could look directly into her eyes and he said quietly, 'We've both had a long and difficult day. Why don't we go and wind down with a meal and a bottle of wine, and celebrate the outcome? It's way past time when you should have been going home and you must be hungry by now.'

The invitation was unexpected and deliciously tempting, but in that short space of time when he had gently put her away from him, her mind had shifted. All at once, she remembered what she had said to Jessica that morning, and she began to panic a little.

'I can't,' she said, her tone suddenly anxious. 'I shouldn't be here. I promised Jessica that I would get back for her. She was so upset this morning when…'

Her voice trailed off. She couldn't go into that now.

'I have to get home… I said that I would make supper for her and Chloe, and she'll be waiting for me. She'll be wondering what's happened to me.'

'Don't you think you've given enough of your time to Jessica and her little girl these last few weeks?' he murmured. 'I know that you worry about her, and that's only natural, but your brother is home now and he'll be looking after them, won't he? Surely you should be able to think of your own needs sometimes? You could do with a break, a chance to let your hair down a bit. Why don't you phone her and tell her something's come up? You'll probably find that she's looking forward to being with Daniel.'

Abby shot him a quick look. 'If I wanted a break, I would have one. I've already told Jessica that I'll see her tonight, and that's what I'm going to do. I'm sorry if that doesn't fit in with your plans.'

His jaw tightened, and she knew that it would be better to explain things to him, but that would only lead to more problems. If he knew that Daniel had gone back to South America, leaving her in the house on her own, he might start pressurising her to move back to the hospital again, and how could she do that and leave Jessica in the lurch?

For the same reason, she couldn't invite him to join them for supper. That way, he would be bound to find out that Daniel wasn't there, wouldn't he? Besides, she knew that Jessica wouldn't want a man around to witness her unhappiness.

'I must go,' she said urgently. 'I'm late already…'

He let her go, his arms falling to his sides, and she turned and fled from the room. He didn't understand at all, that was plain to see, but she was too wary of his reaction to even begin to tell him the truth.

Jessica was relieved when Abby returned home half an hour later. 'I thought you had forgotten,' she said. 'I'm so glad you're back. It's been such a long day.'

'I'm sorry. I was delayed,' Abby said, and told her about the little boy. They went into Abby's kitchen and she made supper, with Jessica's help, while Chloe sat at the table and played tea parties with her dolls. Abby tried not to think about what Jordan must be making of her hasty retreat.

Jessica was much more cheerful after an hour or so, and they moved into the living room and were sipping at glasses of sparkling wine when the doorbell rang.

'Are you expecting someone?' Jessica asked.

Abby shook her head. 'Not really, but I suppose it could be Corinne, back from her sister's house. She said she might pop in if it wasn't too late.'

She went out into the hallway and saw the shadows of two people in the glass panel of the door. Frowning a little, she opened the door and saw two strangers, a man and a woman, standing on her doorstep.

'Can I help you?' she asked. They were an older couple, around their late fifties or early sixties, she guessed, the woman dark-haired, the man with a sprinkling of grey at his temples.

'We were looking for Daniel…Daniel Curtis,' the woman explained. 'Is it possible for us to talk to him?'

'He isn't here right now,' Abby said. 'I'm his sister. Can I help?'

The woman looked at her companion. 'I'm not sure. We're…we're Jessica's parents, you see. Your brother left a message for us, but we were away on holiday, and we couldn't get back to him until now.'

'Come in,' Abby said, standing back to allow them into the hallway. 'I'm really glad you decided to get in touch. I know that there was a problem between you and Jessica, and that you haven't seen her for a number of years, but I hope that it can all be sorted out now. She's been ill, in hospital, and I think she could do with her family around her.'

She wasn't sure what Jessica's reaction would be, but her parents had made the effort to come and see her after all this time, and Abby steeled herself to act as a go-between, or mediator, or whatever was required.

'Come through to the living room,' she said.

She showed them into the lounge, and there was an air of shocked surprise all round as Jessica and her parents confronted each other. Jessica didn't move for a moment from where she was sitting on the settee, and it was only Chloe who said timidly, 'Hello.' Then she went to her mother for reassurance, and Jessica absently put an arm around her.

Jessica's mother looked shaken for a moment, but quickly recovered. 'Hello,' she said to the little girl, then to Jessica she said, 'Oh, Jessica, is she yours? You have a child? I had no idea.'

'Her name's Chloe.'

'How old is she?'

'She's four.'

Her mother looked terribly shaken, but managed to keep a grip on herself. 'It's been so long…so many years,' she whispered. 'I've wanted to see you for such a long time. We had no idea where you had moved to and if it hadn't been for your friend Daniel, we might never have found you again.' She darted a quick, imploring look at her husband, and a silent message winged between them.

Jessica's father cleared his throat and said, 'I know things were difficult between us, but we only wanted the best for you. We…I…thought you were heading for trouble and we wanted to stop you from doing anything foolish.'

He hesitated, looking uncomfortable, then went on gruffly, 'Perhaps I went too far in the things I said. I didn't think it would mean that we would lose you altogether. I hadn't intended for things to work out that way.'

'What your dad means is that we're sorry for what happened,' Jessica's mother said. 'These last few years have been terrible. I've missed you so much.'

She went and sat down next to Jessica on the settee and tentatively rested her hand on her daughter's arm.

Jessica sent her father a cautious look, and then turned to her mother. 'I know, Mum. Me, too.'

Abby made a discreet withdrawal from the room. There were things that needed to be said, and perhaps it was for the best if she gave them all some space. She switched on the kettle and thought about the events of the day.

If only Jordan was here, she would feel so much happier about things but, as it was, she had set herself up for disappointment, hadn't she? She hadn't been sure enough of him to allow her to confide in him, and what must he be thinking of her now?

She took a tray of coffee and biscuits into the living room a little while later, and though the atmosphere was still a little strained, at least they were all talking to each other.

Chloe seemed bewildered by what was going on and sidled warily up to Abby, an anxious expression on her little face.

'I think it's all going to be all right,' Abby told her gently. 'These people are your mother's family, and I think they love you and your mother very much.'

'They not like my daddy?' Chloe asked, and Abby sighed inwardly. How difficult could life get? It was all too easy for adults to forget that children listened avidly to what was being said and then struggled to make sense of it.

'I think they wanted your mummy to be safe,' she explained. 'Sometimes grown-ups get things wrong.'

Jessica and her parents talked to each other for another half hour or so, and then Jessica said quietly to them, 'It's getting late, and it's already past Chloe's bedtime. I need to go and get her settled. Shall we go to my house, next door? It's only a small place, but I think I could put you up for the night if Chloe and I share her room.'

They left together a few minutes later and Abby cleared away the coffee-cups and tidied up. The house seemed empty now that they had all gone, abandoned even by its owner, almost as though it was as cold and lonely as she was feeling inside.

She wondered how Daniel was getting on. Was his flight going smoothly?

Perhaps he had managed to leave a message on the answering-machine. If he had, his friendly voice might help to cheer her up a little. She went and checked and found that there was one message for her, and she sat down and listened to it.

A chill went through her, though, when she heard Richard's voice.

'I saw you with him last night, Abby…that doctor friend of yours. How could you do that to me? How could you kiss another man, when you know that you belong to me?

'I saw you go off with your brother this morning. You went to the airport, didn't you? You know that it would be a mistake to invite your friend back to your house now that your brother's gone, don't you? I won't let it happen, Abby. You should know that I won't let him muscle in where he doesn't belong. You're mine, and I won't let anyone take you from me. I'd kill him rather than let him do that.'

Abby felt sick as she put the receiver down. So Richard had been watching them last night when they had been standing in the porch. She hadn't been imagining things.

Nausea clawed at her throat, and she began to shake uncontrollably. Richard was never going to let her go, was he? He had followed her here from London, and he was still watching her every move. The thought made her shudder.

What could she do to get him out of her life? Perhaps, if she were to confront him, if she could once again tell him that he was wasting his time, this nightmare would be over. But she had tried that already, hadn't she? He had changed his phone number and there was no way of contacting him, other than waiting for him to appear.

That thought filled her with dread. He had been violent in the past and who could know what he was capable of?

The shrill ringing tones of the phone made her jump. She stared at it for a moment. Was that Richard now?

Hesitating, she reached for the phone, and pulled in a shaky breath while she tried to compose herself.

It wasn't Richard. Instead, Jordan's voice came over the line, his voice deep and intensely comforting.

'Abby?' he said, but she couldn't speak for a moment. She was still racked by the shock of hearing Richard's message. 'Are you there?'

'I'm…I'm here.'

'You sound odd. Aren't you feeling well?'

'I'm all right.' She paused, trying to conquer the trembling of her limbs. 'What did you want?'

'You don't sound all right. I know you were shaken up by what happened at work today, but then you rushed off and we didn't have time to talk properly. I've been thinking about it, and I have the feeling that something's not quite right. Are you having more problems with Richard?'

'I told you. I'm all right. I just…I just had supper with Jessica.'

'I thought you would. That's why I left it till later to call you.' He hesitated, then said decisively, 'Look, I'm coming over to see you. You sound really wound up about something, and I'm going to come and find out what it is.'

'No.' The word came out more sharply than she had intended, and she said again, in a calmer tone, 'No, please, don't do that.'

She had to stop him. If Richard was prowling around, he would see Jordan arrive and then anything could happen. He had already hurt her neighbour back in London, breaking his arm, and she couldn't bear it if anything happened to Jordan because of her.

She braced herself to be firm. 'I don't want you to come here,' she said. 'I can look after myself.'

'Even so,' Jordan said, 'I want to.'

'I told you to stay away.' Desperate now, she tried to think of a way to stop him. 'Don't you understand? I've had enough of people interfering in my life. First my uncle, telling me what to do, when to come in, who I could see and who I couldn't see, and then Richard.'

Her voice threatened to crumble, and she fought against it, tensing her shoulders, her neck, her mouth, fighting to get the words out without giving herself away. 'Why can't you get the message? I don't need you coming to watch over me, telling me where I should live, how I should run my life. I want you to leave me alone.'

Abby put the receiver down with a crash and then stared at it, her whole body trembling, the tears coursing down her cheeks.

He wouldn't come now. There was no chance of that. She had lashed out at him and he wouldn't ever want to see her again.

CHAPTER TEN

ABBY wasn't sure how long she sat there, but after a while, when she was empty of tears, she got up and went to the bathroom to splash her face with water.

As she came downstairs again, she heard a knock at the kitchen door, and when she tentatively opened it, she was surprised to see Chloe standing there.

'Hello, Chloe,' she managed. 'I thought you would be in bed by now.'

'I forgot my dolly,' the little girl said. 'I can't go to bed without my dolly.'

'Of course you can't. Let's go and find her, shall we? She must be in the living room.'

She took her through to the room and made a quick search.

'Did you know,' Chloe said importantly, 'I've got a nanna and grandad now? They're sleeping at my house tonight, 'cause they live too far 'way.'

'I know they are. That's nice for you, isn't it?' Abby moved a cushion on the settee. 'Here's your dolly,' she murmured. 'She was fast asleep on the settee all the time.'

Chloe yawned and clutched the doll to her chest. ''Night, Abby.'

'Goodnight, sweetheart.' Abby held her hand and took her back to the kitchen. She would see her back to her own house, but just as she was about to do that, Jessica appeared. 'Oh, she found her doll, then... good. Sorry to trouble you again, Abby.'

'That's all right. Is everything working out all right for you with your parents?'

Jessica grimaced. 'I'm not sure yet. There's a lot we need to sort out.' The front doorbell sounded just then, and she said, 'You go and answer your door— I'll take Chloe home and get her to bed. It's way past her time, with one thing and another. I'll talk to you later.'

Hand in hand, Jessica and Chloe went to the kitchen door and let themselves out, while Abby went along the hallway to the front of the house, a frown working its way into her brow. What should she do if it was Richard out there?

Perhaps this was her chance to tell him once and for all that their relationship was well and truly over. Somehow she had to make him see sense. She couldn't let him go on frightening her and ruining her life for ever, could she?

It was Jordan, though, who was standing in the porch, and as soon as she saw him her panic returned. What if Richard was watching the house even now? 'I asked you not to come here,' she said. 'Please, Jordan, go away. I want you to go.'

His glance flicked over her, his blue-grey eyes cool and unreadable. 'I don't think so.'

He pushed past her into the hallway. 'I'm not going anywhere until you tell me what's going on.'

He shut the door and put a hand in the small of her back, urging her into the living room. 'You're afraid of something, and I want to know what it is.'

'I'm not afraid,' she said in desperation. 'I don't want you here. You must go, Jordan.'

'Maybe I'll go in a while, when you and I have

talked.' He looked her over once more. 'You're not yourself.'

'That's hardly surprising, is it?' she said, attempting a note of scorn. 'I've had a difficult day, one way and another, and now I'm tired.'

'Your brother isn't here, is he? He's gone back to South America and you didn't want me to know.' His gaze narrowed on her. 'Did you think that I would try to take you away from here, pressure you into doing something that you didn't want to do?'

'Yes…something like that,' she admitted. 'And I would have been right, wouldn't I?'

'I'm not like him…I'm not like Richard. It's time you realised that. I want what's best for you, yes, but I would never force you into something that you didn't want. I only want to help, in any way I can.'

'Well, you can help by going away again. I've had a long day and a difficult evening. Jessica and her parents have been here, trying to sort out everything that went wrong in their lives, and things are awkward between them and I've had to try to keep the peace. The only thing that I want now is to go to bed.'

He gave a soft laugh at that. 'Well, at least we're agreed on something. If you gave me only half a chance that's exactly where we would be.'

Her eyes widened, and she stared at him, uncertainty growing in her green gaze.

'Don't tell me that you didn't know that's how I feel about you?' he murmured. 'I want you, Abby, and sometimes when you're in my arms I think that you want me, too. What I find hard to understand is why you keep on fighting me.'

He came towards her and gently laid his hands on her shoulders, caressing her lightly with his fingertips.

More than anything, she wanted to snuggle up against him and have him hold her tightly and soothe away all the worries of the day. She longed to feel the strength and warmth of his body next to hers, but it was too worrying to think what might happen if Richard was anywhere around.

She put a hand shakily against his chest to ward him off. 'Jordan, I tried to tell you not to come here. Why aren't you listening to me? '

'Because I care about you, Abby, and I know that you're hiding something from me. Why won't you let me help you?' His arms slid around her, pulling her into the warmth of his embrace, and her senses started clamouring all at once, chaotically vying with each other in frank appreciation of having him near.

She looked up at him, her green eyes troubled. 'You don't know how difficult this is for me. '

Then she heard a faint sound, and she looked beyond Jordan towards the direction it had come from. On the periphery of her vision there was a movement, a shadow that flitted across the far side of the living room.

Jordan turned at the same moment, following the direction of her gaze. Abby's eyes widened and she gave a gasp of alarm, her nervous system erupting in sudden apprehension. Richard was moving stealthily along the side of the room, and he came to a halt by the curtained window, staring at them, his eyes dark and menacing.

'How did you get in here?' she asked, her voice thick with shock.

'You didn't lock your back door,' Richard answered coldly. 'I took it as an invitation.' He started purposefully towards them, a scowl tightening his features. Moving faster than she had imagined possible, Jordan placed himself in front of her, protecting her.

He said softly, 'So…you must be Richard. I wondered when I would finally get to meet you.'

'Finally…' Richard spat the word out. 'Yes, that's right. Finally is just about the right way to put it. This is the very last time you'll trespass on my territory.' He stood still for a moment, sizing up the opposition. 'She doesn't want you. She's mine. She's always been mine.'

Jordan shook his head. 'You're wrong. Abby has finished with you. She moved here to get away from you. It's time that you understood that, Richard.'

'She'll never leave me.' Enraged, Richard kicked the coffee-table out of the way, sending it crashing into the wall, then flung himself at Jordan, his arms shooting out to grab hold of him and wrench him away from her.

He was a strong man, fit and athletic, his muscles honed by regular exercise in the gym, and Abby was terribly fearful of what might happen if he got hold of Jordan.

Jordan expertly countered his move, though, blocking Richard's hands with a twist of his body and deftly undermining his balance with a well-positioned jerk of his leg.

Richard recovered quickly enough, his fury mounting and firing him into even more aggressive tactics. Jordan stood his ground, countering the attack with a skill and strength that Abby wouldn't have believed possible. Perhaps Jordan worked out in the gym, too. He had always been gentle and kind with her, and she had never seen him this way before, dangerous and determined, his body tensed and ready for action.

Even so, Richard had left a man with a broken limb once before, and she couldn't bear to stand by and do nothing. When Richard lifted the coffee-table and tried to ram it into Jordan's chest, she grabbed hold of Richard's jacket and tried to drag him away. He twisted around and pushed her violently, sending her sprawling across the floor.

Jordan was on him in a second, but Richard aimed a punch at his jaw and landed a cracking blow on his cheekbone. Abby got to her feet and tried to lunge at Richard once more, but Jordan had hold of him by then and swung him away from her.

What should she do? It was clear that she was no match for Richard, and all her efforts to keep him away from Jordan were proving to be useless. He was like a madman, driven, his strength fired by adrenaline and a frenzied desire to win.

If she could just get to the phone and talk to the police...

Richard stopped her before she could reach the extension. He barred her way, and would have grabbed her by the throat if it hadn't been for Jordan dragging him off her.

Now they were both blocking her way, and as the fight went on she was growing more and more desperate.

It was all over a few minutes later. One moment the two men were locked in combat, the next Richard was lying on his front with his arms behind his back and Jordan was straddling his legs and keeping a firm grip on his wrists.

'A length of twine would come in handy,' Jordan said, his breathing laboured.

She nodded. 'I'll get some.'

She started towards the kitchen, but just then there was the sound of rapping on the front door and a deep voice called out, 'Police. Are you there, Dr Curtis?'

Abby was bewildered. She hadn't even managed to get to the phone, so what were they doing there? Then Jessica put her head around the back door, and Abby said, 'Stay there, Jessica. There's been some trouble. I don't want to risk you getting hurt.'

'I know,' Jessica said, coming into the kitchen anyway. 'I saw a strange man coming into your house. He was acting suspiciously, so I phoned the police.'

Abby let out a sigh of relief. 'Bless you. I'll go and let them in.'

She rushed to answer the door, conscious that Jordan was still grappling with Richard, and she wasn't sure how much longer he would be able to hold onto him. Richard had looked subdued, but it could have been an act.

There were two police officers on her doorstep, a man and a woman.

'What's been going on here?' the policeman asked when he walked into the living room. He looked around and saw the broken coffee table and ornaments that had been shattered in the skirmish, and Abby hurried to explain.

Within moments, Richard was handcuffed and led away to the police car outside, and Abby gave more details to the policewoman.

'You say you've had an e-mail and a telephone message from him,' the woman officer said. 'They could be useful if a prosecution is brought against him. Have you kept them?'

Abby nodded. 'I have. I can let you have them.'

'Good.'

Abby said doubtfully, 'I'm not sure whether a prosecution will do any good in the long run. If it went to court and he was served with an order to keep away, I don't think it would make any difference. I've been telling him to do that for a long time now, and he still came after me.'

'Could you get a psychiatrist to talk to him?' Jordan asked. 'I think he needs to see a professional who can get him to understand the root cause of his obsession and to help him deal with his aggression. Perhaps with treatment he'll be able to get on with his life without involving Abby.'

'I'll have a word with the police surgeon,' the officer promised. 'I'm sure he can arrange for something like that to be organised. With a court order and psychiatric assessment, you should eventually see some results.'

'Thank you.' Abby saw her to the door and watched as they drove off. Then she went back to the living room, feeling shaky in the aftermath of all that had happened.

Jordan put an arm around her and hugged her. 'Why don't you sit down? I'll get you something to drink, if you like. Have you got any brandy in the cupboard? It might help to calm you down.'

'I'm all right.' She looked at Jessica who was still there, having waited to see the outcome. 'I'm so glad you saw what was happening. I can't believe how lucky it was that you were there just at the right moment.'

'It was, I suppose, though the noise would have brought me round here anyway,' Jessica said. 'I put Chloe to bed and settled her down, and I thought I saw someone lurking in the garden when I drew the curtains. I thought it might be my ex-husband, and that worried me, so I pressed the alarm. It was only when I saw him coming to your house that I realised who it must be.'

'I'm sorry if we worried you,' Jordan said. 'You have problems of your own, and you've had enough to deal with just lately.'

'I'm all right now. I know that Daniel will be coming back soon, and it looks as though all the arguments with my parents will be smoothed over eventually. My only worry is my ex, but once he sees that Daniel is with me I think he'll stay away.' She made a faint smile. 'My father thinks that between us we might be able to find a way to deal with him, anyway. If we could persuade him to get help for his drink problem, it might solve everything.'

'It's possible.' Jordan put an arm lightly around her shoulders. 'I could arrange for him to get medical help, provided that he's willing, and if you ever need help, you can call on me. I didn't realise that Daniel wasn't here any more, or I would have offered before now. If you need a place to stay, or anything at all, just let me know.'

She smiled and said, 'Thanks. You're very kind...' She turned to Abby. 'Both of you. And I will bear it in mind. But now it's late, and I'm going to go home now and leave you two alone. I'll talk to you tomorrow, Abby.'

'OK, Jessica. Thanks for everything you've done. I'll see you out.'

Abby came back into the living room a few minutes later, and saw that Jordan had made a start on clearing up.

'I'm sorry about all the damage,' he said.

'It's hardly your fault,' Abby told him, going over to him and putting her arms around him. 'I don't know what I would have done if you hadn't been here. You were wonderful.'

'You knew he might come here, didn't you? That's why you tried to keep me away.'

She looked at him, her eyes troubled. 'I was so afraid that he would hurt you.' She reached up and traced the line of his cheekbone with her finger. 'He hit you there. It's a deep cut…you should let me put a stitch in it. Go and sit down at the kitchen table and I'll get a suture kit.'

'It can wait.'

'No. It won't. I want to clean it up for you. I don't want you getting an infection on top of everything else.'

Reluctantly, he did as she asked and followed her into the kitchen, pulling out a chair and watching her as she busied herself making preparations.

'I don't think it will leave a scar,' she said. 'I'll put in three or four stitches and then you'll be almost as good as new.'

Carefully, she cleaned the wound, and then anaesthetised the area before putting in the sutures. 'I don't know how you're going to explain this away at work,' she said, when she had finished.

'At least I've the weekend to think about what I'm going to say,' he said with a smile. 'You're off duty, too, aren't you?'

'Yes. I'd forgotten about that after everything that's happened today. It's been one crisis after another.' She tidied things away, and then stood with her back to the worktop, looking at him. 'You were hurt be-

cause of me,' she said, 'and I feel awful about that.
It should never have happened.'

'You should have told me that Richard had phoned
you,' he told her, his expression serious. 'I've known
all along that he was probably unstable, but I wanted
to be able to protect you. Why wouldn't you let me
do that?'

'I ought to have been able to sort things out for
myself. It isn't your problem, is it?'

'I'm making it mine.' He got to his feet and went
over to her, drawing her into his arms. 'I love you,
Abby, and I want to take care of you. Don't you know
that? Don't you love me at least a little?'

'I was afraid,' she said huskily. 'I wasn't sure that
I could trust my feelings. My instincts were all wrong
in the past, and I was scared that I would make the
same mistakes all over again.'

'And that's why you've been trying to keep me at
arm's length all this time?' His gaze drifted over her.
'At first, I thought it was because we have to work
together, because people would guess what was going
on and there might be talk.'

'It's true, though, isn't it?' Abby said softly. 'You're
a consultant, and I've only been in the department a
short time. People are bound to talk.'

He smiled wryly. 'Do you really think I haven't
considered all that? I have, especially that night when
I saw you settled in at the flat. I wanted to stay with
you, but I thought it might cause problems for you,
and at the same time I didn't want you to feel that I
was taking advantage of you when you were vulnerable. For myself, I don't care what people say. I love
you, and that's an end to it.'

He gazed down into her eyes. 'The fact that people

might talk wasn't your only worry, though, was it? You were anxious about the way things were going with Richard, and it made you uneasy about letting yourself care for anyone.'

'It's taken me a long while to get over the mistake I'd made. Every time you tried to help me I kept wondering if you were trying to take control just like he did. He did it so insidiously that I hadn't realised it was happening until it was too late, and I was frightened that the same thing would happen again. Seeing him again tonight, though, I realise just how unstable he is. '

She trailed her fingers over his chest. 'I know that you're nothing like him. You're strong and confident and you make me feel so good when I'm with you. I know that you'll always be there for me when I need you, and that's a wonderful feeling. I love you so much, Jordan. I just wish it hadn't taken me so long to see what was there in front of my eyes for so long.'

A shuddery sigh of satisfaction rumbled in his throat. 'It seems as though I've waited for ever to hear you say that. I want you, Abby. I need you... I want to be with you always, to talk to you, to feel your body next to mine.'

He bent his head and claimed her mouth with his own, and her defences collapsed like a house of cards, all the hidden longings that had been pent up inside her for such a long time stirred by the tantalising feel of his lips on hers.

She returned the kiss, her fingers reaching up to tremulously explore the hard expanse of his chest, gliding upwards to sensually trace the hard line of his jaw.

The kiss went on and on, became more demanding,

more heart-warming with every second that passed. Jordan's hand stroked the curve of her hip, his body pressing her back against the wall, his fingers moving upwards to discover the soft fullness of her breast.

A soft, pleasurable sigh escaped her, and she heard Jordan's groan of appreciation as his lips explored the silken column of her throat. 'I knew that this was how it could be,' he said thickly. 'I've wanted to kiss you like this, to hold you, to make you mine, almost since the first time we met.' His thumb gently explored the line of her cheek. 'But I'm not being fair to you, am I? You've been through so much, lately…and I should give you time to get over everything that's happened.'

She looked up at him, anxiety clouding her eyes. 'You aren't thinking of leaving me? Please, don't go, Jordan. I want you to stay here, with me.'

'Are you sure? Are you still scared? You shouldn't be—I won't let anyone hurt you. You won't ever need to feel afraid again. I'll take care of you, I promise,' he said huskily, kissing her lips, her cheeks, her throat as though he couldn't get enough of her.

She responded with equal fervour, her mind whirling with the thrill of having him near. 'I'm not afraid,' she murmured. 'I just need you to be here with me.'

He smiled down into her eyes. 'You don't know how much I want to stay. I don't think I could bear to let you go again. I love you, Abby.'

'Show me,' she whispered. 'Make me know it through and through.'

He did exactly as she asked, tenderly exploring the soft contours of her body, his hands and lips caressing her so that she lost all sense of time and place, and simply gloried in the sensual delight of their shared passion.

In the morning, the sun's rays woke her, filtering through the curtains at her bedroom window, and when she looked around, Jordan was still there, sitting on the bed, watching her, a smile playing around his lips.

'So you're awake at last, sleepyhead,' he said softly. His lips brushed hers, rousing her senses in delicious expectation. 'It's such a beautiful day, I thought we might have breakfast and then go down to the beach...unless you have other ideas, of course?'

She wound her arms around his neck and drew him to her. 'That sounds wonderful to me...but there's no rush, is there? We'll have a lazy breakfast-time, shall we?'

He agreed wholeheartedly, and they spent the whole weekend together, doing very little except to revel in each other's company and enjoy the sun and sand. They walked hand in hand along the beach, and just seeing Jordan's easy smile was enough to make Abby's heart thud with contentment.

'It feels so good just being with you,' she said on a ragged sigh. 'I had no idea life could be so full of promise.'

'I'm glad you feel that way,' he murmured, sliding his arm around her waist. 'You look relaxed and happy, as though the sun has kissed all your cares away.'

'I think you're the one who has done that.' She leaned into him, her head resting against his shoulder as they strolled together along the shoreline.

In the weeks that followed, they were with each

other every free moment they could find, either exploring the local coves and hamlets by day or sipping drinks in cosy pubs by night.

One day, Jordan took her to a wide, sun-filled bay, where they had lunch in a glass-walled restaurant on a hillside overlooking the sea. The sky was a clear blue, and the sun warmed them.

'I love it here,' Abby said, as they were finishing off their meal. 'I think it's my favourite place…not just the restaurant but the whole area. From here you can see for miles around, and it's just perfect, so beautiful and peaceful.'

'That's why I brought you here,' Jordan said. 'I thought we might walk along the clifftop after lunch and have a look at the village further inland.'

'I'd like that.' She swallowed the last of her coffee and a few minutes later they made their way out of the restaurant and along the footpath. There were not many people about up here, since most of the holidaymakers had gone back home now that it was term time again.

'I heard from Daniel this morning,' Abby said. 'He says he's planning on coming home next week.'

'That's good news.'

She nodded. 'I think he and Jessica are planning a celebration. It means that I'll start thinking about moving out, though, and finding a place of my own.'

'I knew that you would, sooner or later.' Jordan gave her a searching look. 'I've been doing some thinking myself…'

'Oh? What about?'

'About where you might want to live. There's a place I wanted to show you.'

Puzzled, Abby said, 'What place? Where is it?'

'It's a house that's coming on the market any day now. It's just along here, by the copse of silver birches. I saw it a week or so ago, and I went to enquire about it. I hope you don't mind.' He sent her a quick glance. 'I know the agent—he was brought into A and E some time back in a diabetic coma, and we helped to get him back on his feet. He said I could have the keys so that I could show you the house.'

By now, they had reached the copse, and as they turned around a bend in the winding pathway, the house came into view. Abby gave a soft gasp. It was built of mellowed stone, with a roof set at different angles that added character and charm, and there were windows under the eaves that looked out over the bay. In the front and to the side, the gardens had been lovingly landscaped with flowers and shrubs that added to its appeal.

'It's lovely,' she murmured, still trying to take in what she was seeing.

'I thought you would like it,' Jordan said with a smile. 'Wait till you see the inside. It's everything you could hope for.' He pulled a key out of his pocket and started to unlock the front door. 'The agent said that if we like it, he'll give us first chance to put in an offer.' He pushed open the door and ushered her inside.

'Did you say *we* could put in an offer?' Abby asked, her eyes widening.

'That's what I said.' Jordan looked at her intently, his mouth making a gentle curve. 'We do have a future together, don't we, Abby?' He drew her into the hallway and stood in front of her, his palm resting flatly on the wall beside her head. 'Please, say that we do.'

'I think we do…at least, that's what I hoped for,' she answered huskily. 'These last few weeks have made me realise just how much I want to be with you, always.'

He cupped her face with his hand, and kissed her tenderly. 'I'm so glad to hear you say that. It's what I've been waiting for. That's why I thought about the house. We could live in mine, but I thought you would want a place that we had chosen together.' He held her close, his hands stroking her softly feminine curves. 'You will marry me, won't you, Abby?'

She gazed up at him, her senses thoroughly confused by the delightful way that his fingers trailed over her body, igniting a scorching response from deep within her, but her answer was crystal clear. 'Oh, yes,' she murmured. 'I will marry you.'

'I'll love you for always, you must believe that.'

'I believe you,' she whispered. 'I love you, too, more than you could ever imagine. And you know, as much as I like this house, it won't matter to me where we live as long as we're together.'

'We'll be together for always, I promise.'

She smiled up at him. 'We'll be good for each other, won't we, Jordan?'

'Definitely, we will be,' he murmured, and bent his head to kiss her again. 'Let me show you just how good we can be together.'

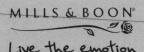

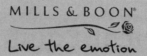

MILLS & BOON®

Live the emotion

Medical Romance™

THE MIDWIFE'S COURAGE *by Lilian Darcy*

Delivering babies all day while knowing she could never have one of her own was hard for midwife Katherine McConnell. Harder still was discovering on her first date with obstetrician Gian Di Luzio that he wanted kids. She had to stop the affair before it even got started. But Gian wanted to be with her above all else…

THE DOCTOR'S CHRISTMAS GIFT
by Jennifer Taylor

Love and family had never been in Dr Catherine Lewis's career plan. But working with Dr Matt Fielding, and playing with his two beautiful daughters, she experiences everything she'd thought she never wanted. As Christmas approaches she must decide if she can she take the risk of a lifetime in Matt's loving arms…

THE SPECIALIST'S SECRET *by Gill Sanderson*

The post of specialist registrar at Dell Owen Hospital means a new life for Dr Alex Storm. He is determined to make an impact on the A&E department – and on Charge Nurse Sam Burns in particular! Sam is certain they could have a magical future – Alex may be secretive about his past but no matter what, Sam is determined that they are going to get through it together!

On sale 7th November 2003

Available at most branches of WHSmith, Tesco, Martins, Borders, Eason, Sainsbury's and all good paperback bookshops.

1003/03b

4 FREE

books and a surprise gift!

We would like to take this opportunity to thank you for reading this Mills & Boon® book by offering you the chance to take FOUR more specially selected titles from the Medical Romance™ series absolutely FREE! We're also making this offer to introduce you to the benefits of the Reader Service™—

* ★ FREE home delivery
* ★ FREE gifts and competitions
* ★ FREE monthly Newsletter
* ★ Exclusive Reader Service discount
* ★ Books available before they're in the shops

Accepting these FREE books and gift places you under no obligation to buy, you may cancel at any time, even after receiving your free shipment. Simply complete your details below and return the entire page to the address below. *You don't even need a stamp!*

YES! Please send me 4 free Medical Romance books and a surprise gift. I understand that unless you hear from me, I will receive 6 superb new titles every month for just £2.60 each, postage and packing free. I am under no obligation to purchase any books and may cancel my subscription at any time. The free books and gift will be mine to keep in any case.

M3ZEE

Ms/Mrs/Miss/Mr ....Initials......................................
BLOCK CAPITALS PLEASE

Surname ....

Address ....

....

....Postcode...................................

Send this whole page to to:
UK: FREEPOST CN81, Croydon, CR9 3WZ
EIRE: PO Box 4546, Kilcock, County Kildare (stamp required)

Offer valid in UK and Eire only and not available to current Reader Service subscribers to this series. We reserve the right to refuse an application and applicants must be aged 18 years or over. Only one application per household. Terms and prices subject to change without notice. Offer expires 30th January 2004. As a result of this application, you may receive offers from Harlequin Mills & Boon and other carefully selected companies. If you would prefer not to share in this opportunity please write to The Data Manager at the address above.

Mills & Boon® is a registered trademark owned by Harlequin Mills & Boon Limited.
Medical Romance™ is being used as a trademark.